To My Wife,

CW00457882

This has been an exciting journey for me, and I know I wouldn't be here if it hadn't been for you. You have and continue to, push me to be the very best version of myself, and I love you so much for that. You know all my dreams and goals, and do everything in your power to make it happen. Though I know I would have eventually gotten to this point in my life, I am so glad that it's happened now, and you've been by my side the whole way.

Your Wife,

Leina R. Ussin

Cheater's Never Prosper

By: Leina R. Duncan

Shania

I stared at him, completely mesmerized by his confidence as he looked over the wine menu. The fact that he was ordering a bottle let me know that tonight was *finally* the night! And Lord knows it had been a long time coming! David and I had been dating going on a year now, and I knew the first time I laid eyes on him, I was going to be his wife. Well, the first time I laid eyes on his American Express Black Card, I knew I was going to be his wife.

David owned his own mobile detailing company and had locations all over Louisiana, Mississippi, and Florida. I thought he was going to be one of those penny-pinching brothas who never wanted to spend their money on anything, but he quickly proved me wrong. From day one,

David made it quite clear he had no issues wining and dining me, and I loved every minute of it.

He was literally like the rich guys on TV who would pop up at your house with a new outfit and tell you to get dressed because he was taking you out. I remember the first time he had pulled that stunt on me. He showed up to my house in a blacked-out Hummer limo. He was holding a gorgeous black and gold gown in his hands, with two women standing at his side.

At first, I thought he had something kinky in mind, which I was ready to suck up and get through to make him happy. But, to my excitement, and relief, he said, "We're going to the Zulu Ball tonight."

I immediately reached for my hair which in no way would be done in time to go anywhere, not to mention my makeup! Knowing what I was thinking, David stepped back and allowed the two women to introduce themselves. "Hey, I'm Niecey, and I'll be doing your makeup! This is Tina, and she's going to hook your hair up!"

I remember sitting in my bedroom feeling like a celebrity while these women got me together within an hour. I couldn't help but blush the entire time as both of them reminded me how lucky I was to have a man who would do this for me. And I made damn sure to show him how lucky I felt later on that night!

My mind snapped back to reality as I listened to David order for us. I low key hated that he did that, but knew if I was going to be Mrs. Powell, I needed to get over that quickly. David's eyes met mine and he gave me that sexy ass smile of his. I couldn't wait for dinner to be over so I could sit on that gorgeous ass face. But I forced myself to remain patient. I had been waiting *months* for David to propose, and it was *finally* going to happen. And though I would've preferred him to do it at my favorite place, Commander's Palace, I decided that Ruth's Chris would do.

"You look beautiful tonight, Nia," he complimented. "You said tonight was a *special* night, so I wanted to look my best for you!" I watched as he eyed me up and down, clearly satisfied with the almost-nude dress that he bought for me months ago on one of our many shopping sprees. "Tonight is most *definitely* a special night! I'm surprised I've been able to contain myself this long," he confessed. My heartbeat started to quicken when I thought maybe he wouldn't make me wait till the end of the night. Maybe he would propose before dinner!

I couldn't help but wonder what the ring looked like. I had dropped *plenty* of hints about being in love with a very specific ring in the Vera Wang Love Collection, so there's no way he could mess this up.

"Are you going to tell me, or are you going to make me sweat over here with anticipation?" David laughed nervously and rubbed his hands along his pants pockets. I wanted to push some more, but I felt it was better to let him propose at his own pace. The waiter walked over and began to fill our wine glasses. My nerves demanded that I gulp mine down quickly, but I followed David's lead and sipped slowly.

David took a deep breath and finally reached for my hands. "Nia," he whispered slowly, "We've been dating for quite some time now, and you've been around for a lot. The opening of my business in Miami, Orlando, and Pensacola. Having you by my side, supporting me has meant everything to me, you know that, right?"

"David, there's no other place I'd rather be than by your side!" I could see a look of relief on his face, and I hoped my words would speed up this process. I was ready to get this ring on my finger. "You have no idea how good it feels to hear you say that. Nia, I need to ask you something. I need to know. . ."

My cell phone rang aggressively on the table, blasting one of Drake's songs loudly throughout the restaurant. I immediately silenced the phone and turned back to David. "Sorry about that, what were you saying?"

But before he could speak my phone vibrated. I snatched the phone off the table and dropped it on the floor. Never once taking my eyes off of David. I could tell my phone calls had thrown off the moment and I was determined to get it back on track. "Do you want to get that?" he asked, concerned. I reached for his hands, "I *want* you to ask me your question!" I said, hiding the annoyance in my voice. I don't know who was trying to ruin this moment, but when I finally got to my phone I was going to curse their ass out!

David started looking confused and reached inside his jacket pocket, taking his phone out. "It's your Nana," he said before answering. I squinted my eyes tightly together wondering what that old woman wanted. I was going to *kill* her for ruining this moment for me. "Yes, I understand. We'll be right there!"

David flagged the waiter over and demanded the check. "What's wrong? What happened?" I asked. Seeing him looking anxious was making me nervous. David threw a couple of twenties on the table and assisted me out of my chair. "We have to get to the hospital, Nia. Your grandmother had a heart attack!"

Mara

It stared back at me. Mocking me. Reminding me in so many ways how much of a failure I was. I could hear my family and friends' voices inside my head trying to convince me otherwise. Trying to reassure me of all the accomplishments in my life. Graduating top of my class at Xavier University, starting my very own productive blogging website, and marrying the most sought out lawyer in New Orleans.

He was a partial owner of an attorney's office with his dad. We owned our own home. And most importantly, *we were happy.*

Everything about my life looked amazing on paper, yet this one line stared back at me, reminding me that none of that mattered. None of it. One small red line that simply meant, "**Not Pregnant**," was a reminder that out of everything I had accomplished in my lifetime, the one thing I *wanted* to do, I was failing at. Having a baby.

I tossed the pregnancy test in the trash and washed my hands, trying to give myself a mental pep talk. I had a semi-busy day today, and wallowing over this wasn't an option. We'd just have to try again. A thought that put a grin on my face almost instantly. I walked out of my bathroom into my bedroom where my husband, Greg, still lay peacefully asleep.

Must be nice, I thought. *The benefits of working nine to five!*

Though I completely loved my blogging website, Mara's Moments, it was definitely a hassle to maintain. I started blogging back in college when I would share with other students the best places to buy or rent used books, the best places to study, even the best places to hang out. I had no idea sharing my opinions with people would have turned into a business of its own. But it had, and I am proud to say I am *very* successful. Many name-brand companies would send me their products to test out and share my thoughts with my viewers. Businesses just starting would also send me products before anyone else had even heard of them, just to get my opinion. So, not only am I receiving free merchandise, I'm getting paid to talk about my thoughts on them.

Sounds easy, right? *Wrong!* There's a constant demand for opinions, believe it or not, and everyone seemed to want mine. I was also responsible for reading and sharing feedback from others who may have had a different or similar experience of an item. I didn't want just my voice to be heard, but the voice of others.

There was also research that needed to be done before receiving and testing a product that was sent to me. If it was something I knew I'd never use in my everyday life, like testosterone pills, there was no need for me to waste anyone's time!

I added water to the Keurig in my office and waited for the perfect cup of coffee to be made. I usually started my day off with a bottle of water and a three-mile jog, but my body would be fine with one day off. I pulled the blinds open allowing the sun to beam through. Using as much natural light as possible always motivated me to work longer. I figured as long as I could see the sun, I should be productive.

I headed back to my desk and started opening a few boxes as my computer started up. I had five new products to test today, and before I started fiddling with anything, directions needed to be read.

I was well into the second pamphlet of the second item when I heard Greg's footsteps on the stairs. He swung into my office before heading to the kitchen. "Did you evaporate out of the bed? I didn't even feel you get up," he said, planting a kiss on my forehead. "I'm surprised you could hear anything with all that snoring you were doing. Sometimes I'm convinced I married a bear instead of a man!"

Greg nestled his face inside my neck, "That's 'cause I'm a beast in the bed, girl!"

I laughed and playfully swatted him away. "Go before you're late for your meeting with your dad!" I slapped him on his butt as he walked out and smiled. Though I was still upset about the pregnancy test, I'd be ovulating next month. We could always try again!

Greg

My phone chimed, and a text message from Mara popped up. *"**Good luck Baby!**"*

I took a deep breath as I realized I was going to need a lot more than luck to get through this meeting. But I was going to continue to be optimistic.

I pulled into the parking lot of Robinson and Associates and saw my dad's car was already there. I could feel my nerves slightly begin to unsettle and I repeated to myself over and over again, *Greg, he's just your dad.*

But my mind knew better. I had been working at my father's law firm for five years now, and you would *never* know I was Bryant Robinson's son. Not that I expected him to cut me any slack, I didn't expect to be completely ignored either. During my first year at the firm, I was given a cubicle office surrounded by paralegals who never took me seriously.

In fact, in my first two years, *none* of the attorneys in his office took me seriously either. No matter how many cases I won, they liked to remind me I was still just a rookie. It wasn't until I won a huge contract case two years ago, did anyone begin to notice me. A case that had gone global, and brought much needed positive attention, *and money*, to New Orleans and our firm. A case that had finally gotten me my own office. A case that made me one of the most pursued lawyers in New Orleans.

I was finally receiving the respect I deserved from the law firm to the point my face was the one chosen to advertise the firm on the billboards located on Canal

Street and the high rise going towards New Orleans East. But with all the praise I received from others, I never got my dad's recognition. I simply recieved an email from him saying, "*Good job.*"

Though I'm well aware that I am past my "lets-make-daddy-proud" phase, the need for his acceptance lingered within me and was something I struggled with every time I pulled into the parking of *his* law firm.

"Greg, your father's wrapping up a call and he'll be with us shortly," Arthur said. Arthur was my father's closes friend, and the second oldest attorney working here. Though work wasn't the right word to use. He had long ago retired from actually taking on cases, and was a professor at

Southern University. But now and then my dad would call him in for some legal advice. And clearly, today was that day.

"Send him in, Arthur!"

My dad stood up as I walked in and we shook hands. "Have a seat, Greg," he demanded. It was pointless to try and read his facial expression, or his tone of voice.

My father always reminded me of a skinny version of James Earl Jones. A deep, powerful voice, but a face that showed no emotion. Growing up, people would tease me and say Mufasa was my dad, minus the affection. At least not towards me. I knew my father was capable of love, by the way he treated my mother and sister. It was seeing him in that way, I knew how to be a good husband. And though I didn't receive much warmth from him, he showered my sister with it all. Something I knew I would do if I were to have a little girl.

"How's Mara?" he asked, a glint of excitement in his eyes. "She's doing great, Dad. She was working on some new products as I left the house this morning. Her blog is blooming for her. She's been featured in some magazines and is actually planning on self-publishing a 'How To' book next year."

"That's great! Her working from home is going to be beneficial and save you guys tons on nursery fees. By the way, is she pregnant yet?"

I could feel my body tense up and I tried my best to remain calm. Before leaving the house, I saw the negative pregnancy test in the trash can. I knew my wife was probably currently at home, beating herself up about it all. I wanted to comfort her this morning, and let her know everything was going to be ok. But that speech was fine in the beginning. A year later, I know it's falling on deaf ears.

"We're still working on it, Dad," I said confidently. My dad leaned back and continued to look at me. "Greg, I started this company fifty years ago, intending to leave something for my family. Though your sister clearly has no interest in the legal field, fortunately, you did. What happens after I'm gone?"

I could feel this was a trick question. But knowing there was only one way to respond, I said, "I would hope the company would be left to me, Dad."

My dad and Arthur both exchanged looks that didn't appeal to my future prediction. My father finally sighed and leaned forward. "The thing is, Greg, before I leave this Earth, I need to make sure this company is left in the hands of two Robinsons who are going to continue with my legacy. Kids are possibly not an option for your sister, so that leaves you."

My uneasiness soon turned into annoyance the way my father made it seem like having a kid was a chore on my checklist. But I expected nothing less from him. Since high school, he had made it quite clear he had my life planned out for me. Marrying Mara was the only real decision I had made on my own. And I often wondered if that would've even happened if he hadn't approved of her.

"Fortunately, we have time until we have to concern ourselves with me being absent from this company. But, since you have indicated, you have intentions of taking over, I am turning over a few of my cases to you. It'll be more work, and longer hours, but if this is what you really want, you'll show me."

My father rose and I stood up with him to shake his hand. "Please, send Mara my love."

I watched as my father walked out, never once asking anything about me. I turned to look at Arthur who could see the disappointment in my face. Arthur placed a comforting hand on my shoulder as we proceeded to walk out of the conference room. "Your father *means* well, Greg. He just wants what's best for you and your family."

I watched as my father waved goodbye to everyone else in the office and walked out the door.

"No, Arthur. He thinks he *knows* what's best for me and my family."

Shania

I splashed more water on my face, though I knew the tired expression would still be looking back at me once I looked into the mirror. Lord knows I couldn't wait to get back to my house and sleep in my own bed. And hopefully, today was that day.

I looked over at the hospital bed where Nana was sleeping. She looked so calm and peaceful like she didn't just suffer a heart attack two days ago. David did his best to stay at the hospital with me as long as he could, but he had a business to run. He made sure to call every hour to check-in though. Every time we talked I fought off the urge to remind him he had a question to ask me, figuring now wasn't the best time to get engaged. I couldn't wait for Nana to get out of the hospital so my life could go back to normal.

There was a knock at the door and the nurse's face appeared. "How's Mrs. Comeaux doing?" she asked me. "She's been sleeping for about an hour now. Is there any word on when she'll be released?"

The nurse looked over a few papers she was carrying. "The doctor will be in shortly to check on her. He'll be able to give you better answers than I can. I'll be back in an hour with a lunch menu!"

I waited until she disappeared before letting an annoyed moan escape my lips. The unknowing was driving me insane. That, and trying to sleep on a hospital sofa.

"You can always head home, Nia, if you need to. I know you're tired," Nana spoke out. Her voice was frail and she sounded so tired. Seeing her this way reminded me of how old she was.

Though I knew she wasn't going to live forever, I stopped paying attention to the fact that she was aging. "I'm not leaving you, Nana. If the doctor comes in, someone needs to be able to remember what he's going to tell you to do."

"I had a heart attack, Nia. I didn't lose my hearing," she joked. But I was in no laughing mood. The bar Nana and I owned and worked at, hadn't been opened in two days! Which meant there was *two days* of business we lost out on. And though our clientele wasn't huge, it was the only income either one of us had.

Mama's Place was a bar Nana's grandmother had opened and had been a family-owned business. Well, partially owned. My family had rented the building out since they opened the bar, too naïve to consider buying it since the owner was a friend of the family. They felt as long as the rent was low, everyone was making enough to feed their families. But that would be changing soon.

"How are we feeling young lady?"

A sexy black doctor walked in, wearing a gorgeous smile. I quickly fluffed my hair out, wishing now more than ever, I had my makeup with me. Nana began to sit up and I was immediately by her side to assist her. 'Take it slow, Nana," I said.

"I'm Doctor Henderson, Mrs. Comeaux. I wanted to come in and check on you, and let you know we'll be releasing you tomorrow."

Finally!

"Is there anything she needs to do once she gets home, doctor?" I looked him up and down, eagerly. *Where had he been the past two days?*

"Yes, as a matter of fact, there is. You are?"

I quickly held my hand out to shake his. "Nia, Nia Comeaux. I'm Mrs. Comeaux's granddaughter. I'll be taking care of her once we leave here."

Doctor Henderson nodded in approval. "Good! She's going to need plenty of rest. I'm going to prescribe her some medicine she's going to need to take daily, and we need to make sure she's as stress-free as possible!"

"That means no more working at the bar, Nana!" I informed her. "She works at a bar?" Doctor Henderson asked, disturbed.

"We *own* a bar, down in Chalmette. It's called Mama's Place. Ever been?"

"I'm afraid I don't make it to that part of the city often." I took a step closer to him. "Well, maybe now you have a reason too."

"Uh, we'll see, Miss Comeaux." I watched as he completely bypassed me and made his way to Nana's bed.

"Here are the different activities I want you to start doing. I'll have the nurse start you on your diet today, just so you can get into the swing of things. Tomorrow she's going to discharge you with all of this information, as well as my contact info. Please, Mrs. Comeaux, if *anything* comes up, you let me know!"

Nana took all of the paperwork and placed it on the chair next to her bed.

"Thank you, doctor. I'm looking forward to going home."

I waited for him to turn around and acknowledge me still standing there. He didn't. *Uptight ass*, I thought to myself.

My phone buzzed in my back pocket and I smiled when I saw it was David calling. "Hello, handsome! You must know I miss you!"

"Hey Beautiful, how's Nana doing?" I glanced her way as she readjusted herself to lay down. "She's doing amazing! The doctors are releasing her tomorrow!"

"That's great, Nia! I'm *really* glad to hear that!"

I stepped inside the bathroom and closed the door behind me. "I would *really* like to see you tomorrow night! It's been so long since I've been close to you," I whispered to him. I listened as David took a deep breath in and sighed into the phone. "I would *love* that, Nia. But I'm actually on the way to the airport. I'll be in San Antonio for the next couple of weeks."

Weeks????

"San Antonio? Why?" I demanded. I wasn't going to hide the irritation in my voice. I wasn't going to go weeks without seeing him! Too much could happen with him in another state for weeks. "That's what I was trying to tell you the other night! I've been looking into expanding my business to Texas, I wanted you to come with me!"

I closed my eyes as I let his words hit me. "*Wait! Wait, wait, wait wait, wait, wait, wait!* So, the other night at dinner, *that's* what you wanted to ask me? To come to Texas with you while you conducted business?"

"*Of course!* This is *huge* for me, Nia! I wanted you to be here for it all!"

An irritated laugh escaped my lips and I wanted to pitch my phone out the bathroom window. "Are you ok?" David asked.

"No, David, I'm *not* ok! I thought you were going to ask me to *marry* you!"

There was silence on the other end, and I could only imagine what David's face looked like. "Nia, I'm-I'm sorry if I gave off the impression that I wanted to get married. But I don't. I thought we were just having fun!"

My hand began shaking as I squeezed the phone tighter and tighter. "Um, look, I'm about to board this plane. How about we take a break for the next couple of weeks and I'll holla at you when I get back to the city. Cool?"

But he didn't give me a chance to respond. He hung up, and I remained in the bathroom, clutching the phone to my ear.

The doorbell rang, completely distracting me from the review I was rapidly typing up. I already knew who it was and she would have to wait. Knowing I was probably wrapped into my work, she began ringing the doorbell back to back. I couldn't help but smile as I typed the last sentence and updated my website.

"If there are *any* grammatical errors I'm kicking your behind," I yelled as I swung the door open. "Girl, we both know you couldn't make any errors even if you typed with your eyes closed!" I watched as my best friend, Porsha, strutted in and handed me a bottle of wine. "Porsha, it's not even noon yet!" I laughed, following her to the kitchen.

She pulled two wine glasses out my cabinet sighing, "It's Happy Hour somewhere, so let's celebrate it now!" I watched as she filled both glasses way passed the standard eight-ounce mark and took a large gulp out of hers. "*Bad day?*" I asked, hitting the nail on the head. "You have *no* idea! *Why* in the hell was I convinced that working for someone was a good idea?" Porsha handed me one of the wine glasses, letting me know I had no choice but to drink with her.

"Come on," I said defeated, leading her to my office. She sat down on the sofa across from my desk and added more wine to her glass. "What's going on?"

"Those people at that magazine know absolutely *nothing* about talent. They think makeup tips and fashion is what people care about, and it's not! I did *not* waste five years of my life going to college and interning to write about the latest trend in fingernail art!"

"Let's be clear," I said jokingly, "it would've been four years if you wouldn't have partied so hard our freshman year!" Porsha threw one of the pillows at me which I was able to quickly dodge. I was glad to see she was laughing though. "Hey, you were boo'd up enough for the both of us with Greg's ass! I, on the other hand, wanted to explore my options before just settling down!"

"Ok, and what's your excuse now, Porsha?" She leaned back and let out an aggravated sigh. "Why every time I bring up my career, you bring up my love life?" I held my hands up innocently. "I'm just saying, you can have both!"

"I'll just live vicariously through you and Greg as of now if you don't mind. I want to focus on my career before I have to worry about babysitting a man!"

"Speaking of babysitting men, my mom is doing her yearly headcount for my dad. Are you coming with us to the Zulu Ball this year?" Porsha dropped her head back and it was evident it had slipped her mind. "I haven't even started *looking* for a gown! Your dad isn't *tired* of going yet?"

"*Are you kidding?*" I chuckled. "You *know* my dad! He's going to go as long he has breath in his lungs! Being on the Board of the Zulu Club means more to him than meeting Obama!" Porsha laughed along with me. I was more than sure she was replaying the conversation we heard once a year, at *every* Zulu Ball, from my dad about the history of the Zulu Club. And even though I could recite the conversation word for word, I had to admit that being a part of such a historically black social club was a big deal. "Let me not complain too much, maybe I'll find my next man there," Porsha teased.

"Please do! I would love for someone to knock you up!" Porsha let out an exasperated sigh and I couldn't help but laugh at her feminist ways. "Excuse me for loving the idea of our kids growing up together being the best of friends!"

Porsha's face suddenly lit up and she walked over towards me. "Wait, *are we pregnant?*" she asked excitedly. I clearly didn't hide the disappointment as well as I thought I did, and she sat down next to my feet. She placed her head on my leg and said, "I'm sorry." I ran my fingers through her locs, trying to convince her, as well as myself, everything would be ok.

"Did you tell Greg yet?"

"No, he has that big meeting with his father today, I didn't want to dampen it with any bad news." Porsha popped her head up looking annoyed. "It's not something *you* should have to carry alone! He wants a baby just as much as you, right?"

"Of course he does. He even went to the doctor to check his sperm count. I'm starting to think it could be me!" I hated the self-doubt I had been feeling lately. I didn't want to burden anyone with the job of consoling me all the time. But Porsha could always see through me and lying to her wasn't worth the effort.

"Listen to me," she said, getting on her knees so we could almost be face to face, "You're the most *amazing* person I know! Everyone knows that, and you know that too! Only about fifteen to twenty percent of couples who try to get pregnant actually do right away! And you guys just need to space out your sex lives and stop going at it like rabbits!"

"Alright *WebMD*," I teased her. "We're aware of all of that. We're damn near down to having sex *only* when I'm ovulating. I'm waiting for Greg to get annoyed and be done with it all!" I confessed. Porsha looked unconvinced. "First of all, that man adores you! Second of all, it would be a cold day in

hell before Greg decides he's done with you!
Now, come on, let's finish this wine!"

Shania

I held down my horn as the light turned green and the car in front of me remained at a stop. It was already pushing 3 o'clock and if I wasn't out of the city by at least 4, I would get caught in the parade traffic.

Chalmette wasn't far from New Orleans at all, but when it came down to festivals or major events in the city, we were two different worlds. And I was convinced *no one* in the city remembered how to drive! It had been a short ride to the attorney's office, but I was still cursing my grandmother out the entire time. She was the one who usually handled our legal affairs, but I'm in charge now that she's on bed rest. *Selfish ass woman!*

I pulled into the parking lot and slipped my jacket on. New Orleans weather was tricky around this time of year, and though it was warm now, it had the potential to drop down to the 60s really quick. I gathered all the necessary documents with me and rushed inside to make my appointment on time. The receptionist greeted me with a smile, but I was not in the mood.

"Shania Comeaux here to see Mr. Gregory Robinson," I announced. The receptionist instructed me to have a seat and my annoyance level rose higher. I glanced down at my watch praying this wouldn't be a thirty-minute wait. I still had to go unlock and set the bar up, and with my grandmother so *conveniently* out of service, it would take double the time to do it. I scrolled through my Facebook feed as I waited.

David hadn't posted anything since he made it to Texas and I was getting impatient. I had tried calling to check-in to see how things were going, but he never returned my calls. The idea of some chick trying to replace me constantly crossed my mind and I *knew* David wasn't the type to resist. Yea, he had been faithful to me while we were together, but that's because we were *together.* But with him thinking we are on some kind of "break" I know I didn't stand a chance against any of the women casually throwing themselves at him while he's gone.

It had only been a few minutes but I couldn't sit still any longer. I began gathering my things so I could head out the door and back to my side of the city. *This shit will have to get done later!*

I was just reaching for my purse when a man called my name, "Mrs. Comeaux?"

Yum-me, I thought to myself. *So this is why Nana would drive her old ass up here to see her attorney instead of finding one closer to home!*

He stood before me like an African God, and I had all the best ways to get on my knees to worship him. There was something about a brotha in a suit that did absolutely *everything* for me. Trying my best not to bite my lip, I managed to say, "It's *Miss* Comeaux. Mrs. Comeaux is my grandmother!" I held my hand out praying to the gods he would kiss it. I needed just a little sample of what those lips felt like. Much to my disappointment, he shook my hand. "It's nice to meet you. I'm Gregory Robinson, won't you follow me, please!"

I followed him to his office taking the opportunity to check out his physique. Broad shoulders, nice size arms, and a nice tight ass. My mind could only guess what he looked like in some grey sweat pants. *Calm down, Nia*! I had to refocus my brain and remind myself of why I was here.

"Please have a seat. Forgive me, my father just handed over your file to me so I'm still catching up. I believe your grandmother just recently had a heart attack?"

"Yes," I said, touching my chest, trying to sound upset. "It took us all by surprise and I've just been simply devastated having to leave her at home alone while I practically run the bar by myself!"

He placed a consoling hand on my shoulder and I had to resist the urge to slip one of those chocolate fingers in my mouth. "I'm sure your grandmother is grateful to have a granddaughter like you!"

I watched as he walked over to his desk and sat down. "So, what brings you here today, I believe your grandmother was saying something about officially buying the bar?"

I reached for the paperwork and slid it over to him. "Yes, the owner is finally looking to sell and made us an offer. But of course, my Nana doesn't do anything without her attorney's approval. So, I offered to come down and bring the paperwork for her." Greg flashed me one of those panty-dropping smiles and I no longer cared how long this meeting took. As he flipped through each page of the contract, I took the opportunity to do some snooping. There were plenty of law books behind him, something I personally believed lawyers did for show.

His diplomas from Xavier and Loyola University were shining brightly behind him like he polished those bad boys daily. My eyes finally fell on his desk. Two picture frames were facing him on an angle, each one with a different woman on them. *Shit.*

"Your wife is beautiful," I said convincingly. Greg looked up at the photo I was speaking of. "Oh, that's my sister, Ashley. But thank you, I'll have to let her know that!" *One down,* I thought to myself, hoping he'd address the second picture. As if reading my mind, he reached for it and turned it over for me to see. "*This* is actually my wife, and I must say she looks better than my sister!" Never once glancing at the photo, I allowed an agreeing laugh to escape my lips as I kicked myself on the inside.

Of course a brotha this fine is married!

My mood had immediately changed and I was ready to go. "Is there any way we could get the suggestions back at a later time? I *do* have to run back to Chalmette to check on my grandmother before opening the bar." Greg understandingly nodded and slid the papers back inside the folder on his desk. "Of course, Miss Comeaux. I'll look over everything tonight, do a little research and get back with you by next week. Or should I call Mrs. Comeaux?"

You're married, who cares who you call!

Keeping the fake smile on my face I casually replied, "Either or would be fine!" I gathered my things and headed out of his office. "Come to think of it, I believe I've passed this place a few times. My wife has family up in Violet!" Since my back was turned I was comfortably able to roll my eyes before turning back to him.

"That's lovely!"

"I might have to stop by there sometime and get a drink!"

I couldn't control the grin spreading across my face as he emphasized 'I' instead of 'we.'

Realizing it was now or never to plant my bait, I swayed my hips seductively back towards him and leaned over, "Well, if *you're* ever in the area, stop by. Your drink will be *on* me!"

Greg

I reached for Mara's hand to relax her, and to stop her from fidgeting with a napkin she had begun to shred into tiny pieces. She glanced my way, giving me an awkward smile. *She's so cute when she's nervous.*

But I was a tad bit nervous myself. We had mentioned being open to going to a doctor if we ended up having fertility issues, but that was when we first discussed having a baby a year ago. I had no clue we would *need* to. Especially after my doctor confirmed I had a great sperm count. But we had tried again around her ovulation period, and weeks later, no baby.

I was extremely hesitant to bring our problems to a doctor, but I wanted some kind of answer, as opposed to knowing nothing at all. "What if it's me?" Mara finally asked, breaking the silence between us.

"What if I'm the reason we can't have our baby?" I could see the tears forming in her eyes and quickly wrapped my arm around her. "*Whatever* it is Mara, we're going to get through this together. Do you understand?" She nodded gratefully as I wiped the tears off her cheeks. I placed a reassuring kiss on her forehead reminding myself that no matter what the doctor said, I needed to be strong for her.

There was a knock on the door, and Doctor Tran walked in smiling. "Mr. and Mrs. Robinson? How are you guys this morning?"

"We'll be doing great if you can tell us why we're not pregnant, Doctor Tran," my wife halfheartedly joked.

"Please, call me Vanessa! I like to be personal with my patients, especially with matters as serious as this one!"

I could see a horrified look on Mara's face, "*Serious*? Is there something wrong with me?"

Vanessa quickly held her hands up. "No, Mrs. Robinson, I'm sorry! I worded that wrong. I meant having a baby is a serious matter! There's nothing more beautiful and important than two people deciding to bring a baby into this world! I want you guys to consider me a doctor and a friend," she said soothingly.

I resisted the urge to roll my eyes as I realized this friendship was costing me $500.

"Please, call me Mara. And this is Greg, my husband," my wife said. We all finally shook hands and Vanessa began flipping through some of the paperwork on her desk. "So, I had your OBGYN fax everything over to me, and Mara, it looks like you're a perfectly healthy woman. And Greg, I am aware you have an amazing sperm count!"

"*So why aren't we pregnant?*" Mara asked, and I could hear a hint of aggravation in her voice. I reached for her hand and gave her a tender squeeze. She had a tendency of getting panic attacks when she got too overwhelmed, and I needed her to remain calm.

"I know you guys feel like something is wrong, but please know that ninety percent of couples get pregnant after they've been trying for *over* a year. So what you guys are experiencing is quite common! But just to make sure there's absolutely nothing wrong, we will do a blood test on you, Mara. I'm going to also schedule you to come back in a few days for an ultrasound. We're going to go ahead and make sure everything is looking great!"

She began jotting some things down before handing it over to us. "I'm going to go ahead and place you on some prenatal vitamins to take as soon as possible. Also, I'm going to place you on, what I like to call a fertility diet. A lot of my patients have followed it and conceived within a few months!"

Mara flipped anxiously through each sheet and I knew she was going to be studying each one as soon as we got home. She slid the papers inside her purse and turned back to Vanessa. "And if this doesn't work, what's next?"

"If *none* of these options end up working, we can always try IVF. Now, I'll be honest, I prefer to use this as a last resort, but it's definitely an option."

"What's IVF?" I asked. Vanessa pulled out some other papers from her desk and handed them over to us. "It's an in vitro fertilization. We would place Mara on medication to produce multiple eggs, retrieve them, inseminate them with your sperm, and once we were sure we had a healthy embryo, we would go ahead and insert it back inside Mara. There's a breakdown of the cost of this procedure on the back of the page."

We rode home in silence, and I knew Mara was still blaming herself for everything. I tried cheering her up after we left the doctor's office and told her I was more than confident everything was going to work out. But I knew we both shared the same concern. The costs.

Yes, we were both doing fine, and could afford the treatment, if it was needed. But we could both agree, neither one of us planned on spending twenty grand on a kid unless it was going towards their college tuition. But it was my job to make sure she didn't stress behind it.

"Since you'll be starting this diet soon, how about I take my best girl out to eat tonight? It can be your last hoorah!"

But Mara continued to stare out the window. It pained me to see my wife so distraught, especially since there was nothing I could do to fix it. We pulled in front of our house and I shut the engine off. But neither one of us made a move to get out. I watched as Mara took a deep breath in and began sobbing hysterically.

Unhooking my seatbelt, I leaned over and embraced my wife as she cried into my arms. "*I just don't understand*," she kept saying, as I rocked her from side to side. I fought back my own tears as I continued to hold her, knowing she was the one who needed this moment. Not me.

She finally pulled back and began wiping her face off. "I don't want to lose you because of this," she confessed. I felt a sting in my chest realizing how much pressure she was putting on herself behind this.

"Mara, there's *nothing* on this Earth that could take me away from you! We're going to have a baby, and I'm going to give both of you the world!"

I grinned when I noticed a smile on her face. "You promise?"

"I promise," I said, kissing her forehead.

"I love the idea of having the world," she said innocently. "But right now, can we start with some crawfish?"

Shania

I pulled in front of my Nana's house trying to prepare myself for her. Not even a heart attack could change how aggravating she was, and I didn't feel like dealing with her and then dealing with a bunch of drunks at a bar. There was an unfamiliar truck parked in the driveway with a Florida license plate, and I immediately got pissed. *The fuck is she doing here?*

I stormed into the house and headed straight to the kitchen. *Not* to my surprise, they were in there, eating like it was Thanksgiving. Nana smiled when she saw me and got up from the table to hug me. But my eye's never left the unwelcomed visitor, who was stuffing her face and smiling back at me. "What's up, Sis," she said, sarcastically. I had every urge to wipe that cocky smile off her face but decided to half-ass hug my grandmother instead.

"What's up, Kissy."

I made my way to the kitchen table and sat down with Nana right behind me. "Isn't this exciting," she said, acting like a child on Christmas. "Both my grandbabies sitting here after so long!"

"It's *just* Kissy, Nana! Stop acting like the Pope is in your house!" I snapped. Nana nonchalantly began fixing me a plate as Kissy glared unapprovingly out the corner of her eye. I could tell she was refraining from causing a scene and turned back to our grandmother. "You're looking good, Nana. How long until I can take you outta here to come check out Florida?"

Nana just giggled as she sat a plate down in front of me. "Girl, ya grandma don't need to be on no beach, as old as my behind is. I need to be right here. Relaxing these old bones."

"Come on, you know you're not a day over 60, Nana! Come show those folks in Florida how a two-piece is supposed to look!" I watched with annoyance as my grandmother continued to laugh at Kissy's nonsense. I slammed my fork down and stood up, deciding I wouldn't be composed anymore!

"What do you *want* Kissy, *huh*? Why are you *here*? To leech off of Nana some more? To take all her money and just disappear for three years?" I could see my words hurt her, but family or not, I could care less. Every time she showed up she left behind some kind of mess for *me* to clean up and I was tired of it.

"I came when I heard about Nana's heart attack, Nia! I'm not here to take money from anyone!" Nana was reaching for my arm to calm me down, but I quickly slapped it away. "I call bullshit! The only time you ever come down here is when there's something in it for you! *What*, you heard she was possibly going to own the building to the bar and you want to secure your cut?"

Kissy slammed her fork down and stood up to be eye level with me. "We all know you don't want me here, Nia, and I promise I'll do my *best* to stay out of your way. But until Nana is back up and running, get used to seeing my face!"

Having enough of this, I snatched up my purse and walked away from the table.

"Kissy, I had no choice but to get use to *that* face a long time ago!"

It was a slow night and I was beyond grateful for it. The brief interaction with my sister and grandmother had ruined any chance of me having a good day. All I wanted to do was close the bar early and go home! I looked around at the regulars who came pretty much every night and sat glued to the slot machines.

If we did get to buy this building, that was going to be the first thing to go. My eyes traveled around the ancient bar my family had started but never bothered to update over the years. I chuckled to myself, *who was I kidding, it's been like centuries*!

"I'm out, Nia, kitchen's cleaned and locked down!"

I waved bye to Jeff, our chef/bouncer, as he headed out. "One for the road?" I asked, already pouring him a shot of vodka. Sliding it down his way, I watched as he caught it and swallowed it down. "Ahhhhhh, best way to end a night. Sure you're good locking up alone?"

I looked around at the four men sitting around who I was more than sure a toddler could take on alone if need be. "Uh, yeah, I think I'm good!" He waved one final goodbye and was out the door. I glanced down at my watch. *Fuck it*, I thought. I flickered the lights twice, making them aware it was last call and I would be shutting it down soon.

"Aww c'mon, Nia. I got a feeling tonight's the night!" I rolled my eyes at Mr. Robert who looked like he had been coming here since this place first opened. He had been such a frequent customer, Nana had reserved him his own slot machine that no one else could touch. "Mr. Robert, I promise you, the day you win on that machine, it'll be you winning back every penny you lost putting in there!"

I watched as the other three men started gathering their things and mumbled out what sounded like a goodbye. I was following them out the door to cut off the open sign that flashed outside, when the bar door swung open, almost knocking my ass down.

"*Hey!*" I shouted, ready to give whoever it was a piece of my mind. I was shocked when I saw Greg's face turn around and smile. "I'm sorry, a gust of wind kinda blew me in!"

I could feel my aggravation quickly vanish and I smiled. "No problem, you just scared me! No one usually comes in this late!"

I watched as he looked around the pretty much empty bar and turned back to me and ask," Closed for the night?" Not wanting him to leave, I quickly took his arm into mine and guided him towards the bar. "Not at all! What can I get you to drink?"

"Crown and coke."

I nodded with delight as I began fixing his drink. "So, what brings you all the way out here, Mr. Robinson? Visiting your in-laws?" If his wife was going to pop in, I needed to be ready. I slid the drink towards him and watched him take a sip. His face lit up and I could tell he liked the secret ingredient I added.

"Hint of lime juice," I confessed before he could ask. He nodded with approval. "This is really good!" I watched as he drank it down and I began fixing him another. "How long have you been bartending?" he asked, watching how well I maneuvered myself behind the bar. "For as long as I can remember, honestly. Making drinks was kind of like a rite of passage in my family. Most girls would go grab their daddy a beer. In my family, we had to learn how to make him a Long Island by the age of ten!"

"Sounds impressive!"

I couldn't help but grin at the memory of me and my father in the kitchen concocting our own drink recipes. "To some, yea, to me, it was just a fun way to spend time with my daddy!"

"I was informed of his passing some time ago. I'm sorry for your loss." I could hear the genuineness in Greg's voice and instantly cleared my throat to avoid getting emotional. "It was a *long* time ago. But I know you didn't come down here to hear about life's story!" I teased, thankful to change the subject.

Greg pulled an envelope out of his jacket and slid it across to me. "I've reviewed over the proposal made to you about buying this place, did some research on the surrounding area, and was able to renegotiate the price for you."

I opened the envelope up and started reading. My eyes widened as I saw the new price. "This is like thirty percent *less* than what he was asking for!" An arrogant smile spread across his face and I had to ignore the urge to take him right then and there on the bar in front of Mr. Robert.

"What can I say, I'm a good negotiator." I immediately began fixing him, as well as myself, a shot. "Cheers to after four generations, the Comeauxs *finally* owning this place!"

We toasted our shot glasses together and tossed the crown down with ease. Greg placed his glass down and stood up. "Well, I just thought I'd deliver the good news in person!"

"Wait," I said, trying to think of any excuse for this man to stay. "The rest of my staff is gone for the night, any way you'd be up for staying a few minutes longer? I'm kinda scared to close up alone!"

Greg looked down at his watch and then back at me. I smiled with delight as he slid his jacket off and sat back down. "Yea, I can swing a few more minutes!"

Mara

I looked down at my husband as he continued to snore, completely oblivious that I was wide awake. Staring at him. It wasn't the snoring that was disturbing me, but the smell of alcohol oozing out of his pores. It was overwhelming and becoming nauseating. I knew Greg would have a drink or two after work, but it wasn't like him to get drunk. Deciding not to ease up on him with this one, I climbed out of the bed and threw our balcony curtains apart.

The sunlight did exactly what I wanted it to do. Smack him in the face and wake him up. Greg struggled to hold his hand up to shield his eyes as he tried to look at me. "What...what time is it?" he stuttered out. "Nine fifteen. You need to get up and make yourself look like something. Keith's brunch is today!"

I walked past him into our bathroom, fully prepared to leave without him if he couldn't get it together in time. I couldn't hide the disappointment in my eyes as he dragged himself into the bathroom behind me and splashed water on his face. Now and then he'd reach for his head and I was more than sure he had a tornado of a headache. Against my better judgment, I grabbed the Tylenol from the medicine cabinet and placed it next to him.

"Take two. I'll go make you some tomato juice after we get out of the shower."

As I played around with the water temperature, I felt his arms around my waist. He placed soft kisses on the back of my neck and I could feel my disappointment with him dwindling. Though the smell of alcohol clung to his skin, he had at least brushed his teeth, and the cool minty taste of his tongue was enough to completely draw me in. After all this time, he could *still* kiss me and make me feel like a little girl, kissing a boy for the very first time. I felt his arms around me, lifting me and easing my body into the shower. I wanted to remind him we both were still fully clothed, but my mouth dared not leave his.

My hands stayed wrapped around his face as he undressed me and tossed my clothes aside. I had wanted to wait until I was closer to my ovulating date before making love again, but I was never able to tell him no. He quickly whirled me around so my back was towards him. I clung to the wall for dear life as he eased my panty's down and devoured me from behind.

My back arched allowing him full access and I could feel him messing with his now drenched pants. I turned around to assist him and he stood up for me. I stared up at him smiling as I tugged his pants and briefs down. I was glad to see he was already hard and waiting for me. Returning the favor, I eased him into my mouth, never breaking eye contact,

His facial expressions motivated me to go harder, moaning so he knew I was enjoying tasting every inch of him. I could feel the back of his legs tense up and he reached down to pull me up. I was back facing the wall and I spread my ass apart as he eased himself inside of me. A pleasurable moan escaped our mouths simultaneously with each thrust, and I knew for sure we were going to climax together. My legs began to buckle under me as I felt the tsunami within me rising. "*Fuck, Mara,*" he moaned out as we climaxed together. I continued to hold on to the wall as my body shook against his. I could still feel him inside of me and knew he felt me pulsating on him. "Damn girl," he breathed into my ear. I smiled as I slowly turned around and kissed him.

"You're going to be the one to explain to Keith why we're late," I demanded. Greg placed soft kisses on my shoulder and I watched as he sneakily began to go lower. "I'll tell him whatever you want as long as you give me one more."

Greg

I smiled walking into Keith's club, seeing all the familiar faces. His family and some friends we went to college with were all here to celebrate his club that would officially be opening tonight. I caught Keith's eyes and he made his way towards me to dap me off. "Finally, I was starting to think ya'll forgot!"

He leaned in and hugged Mara. "You look beautiful as always," he complimented her. Mara smiled. "Keith, you were always the charmer!"

"You know me, the lady's man!" We all laughed knowing that was the furthest thing from the truth. "Well, I see Porsha is here," Mara teased. My wife had tried hooking our best friend's up years ago, against my better judgment. But just like I predicted, it didn't end too well. Keith looked over as Porsha was barking orders at some photographer to take pictures. "Uh, yea, *somehow* she convinced me to do an exclusive about my club for her job. Something about trying to impress her boss."

Mara nodded, "Sounds about right. I will go speak to her." I kissed my wife and watched her disappear into the crowd. "Bruh, have I mentioned how lucky you are," Keith said. I couldn't help but smile. "Yea, I know I am! But how are you doing? How are you remaining so calm knowing in just hours this place is going to be packed?"

Keith sighed anxiously. "Bruh, believe it or not, I am secretly losing my shit! I still can't believe all of this is *really* happening!" Keith looked nervously around the spot he had been dedicating almost a year to fixing up. It was his dream to own his own club, and I was beyond glad that he was finally doing it. "Your mom would be proud," I let him know. Keith nodded and dapped me off. "Thank you man, I appreciate that! Come check out VIP with me!"

The elevator in the back of the club brought us to the second floor to a decked-out area. "I see the interior designer you used worked well for you. You sure it was *all* business?" I asked. Keith laughed as he fixed me a drink from the bar in the VIP area. "Yea, I could sniff she was a climber before she opened her mouth."

He handed me a drink and noticed the confused look on my face. "A climber is a woman, or man, who sees someone on the rise and wants to attach themselves so they can climb up as well. She had a lot going for herself, but I wasn't interested in being her ladder. She can get there on her own!" I nodded as his statement made sense, and we clinked our cups together before tossing our shots down. "Besides, I'm waiting for you to mess up so I can scoop Mara away," he teased.

We simultaneously laughed at the ongoing joke between us. Keith had been around since the beginning of me and Mara, so he knew, just as well as I did, how much of an amazing woman she was. I peered down into the crowd and spotted her laughing at something Porsha was saying. I knew she was still upset about not being pregnant, but she held up very well. She was strong, so strong, and I loved her for it.

"Trust me bruh, I've messed up a lot in life. That's one mistake I'll never make."

Keith turned back and headed back to the bar. I was right behind him as he poured us another shot. "How'd the meeting with your dad go?"

"Don't even ask," I muttered out, tossing back my second shot. "That bad?" Keith asked.

"I pretty much feel like if I *don't* have a kid, there's no way my dad is going to leave me his company!"

"Did he actually *say* that?" Keith asked, and I could tell he thought the idea was just as messed up as I did. "He said it in his own way." I leaned against the bar and let a helpless sigh escape me. "Well, Mara *wants* a baby, and she's not going to stop till she has one, so I wouldn't stress about that at all," Keith said, trying to sound positive.

"It's not Mara I'm worried about, honestly. It's me. In the beginning, when we discussed having kids, I was excited because that's what *I wanted.* Now, it's starting to feel like I have to have a kid because it's what my *dad* wants. I don't want to bring a kid into this world based upon someone else's expectations!"

I put my head down realizing I needed to get it together. I knew I could always come to Keith and vent, but even I realized I was starting to sound emotional. I slid my glass towards him indicating I needed another shot. Without hesitation, he filled my glass up.

"Look, I may not be the best person to advise you since I didn't know my father.

But I know this, I've known you damn near a decade now, and there's no one I know that deserves a kid more than you and Mara! Who cares who's in your ear about it? All that matters is that *you* love your wife, and you'll *love* that kid too!"

I dapped Keith off as he walked around the bar towards me. "Now, if you're quite done with this sensitive shit, I'd like to get back to my party," he teased.

Shania

I watched as Kissy screamed her head off trying to get the attention of the people on the floats. She looked like a lunatic, along with *everyone* else, yelling to have someone throw beads at her. I could feel a form of resentment growing inside of me watching everyone have so much fun. I couldn't help but reminisce on a time when I used to be one of those people! I used to enjoy shouting at the people on the floats as they passed by, trying to catch their attention so they would take pity and throw me something! *Anything!*

I remembered standing on the top of my daddy's ladder, with him right behind me so I wouldn't fall, as I waved frantically to catch a bead! I remembered how he would run along the side of the floats to try and get us stuffed animals every year. That was always his goal, to make sure his daughters left the parades with stuffed animals.

Then he died, and as much as Nana tried to make Mardi Gras fun for us, it was ruined forever for me. And for *years* I had avoided it.

But here I was, at a parade, because somehow I let Kissy convince me to spend time with her. Feeding me all this crap about wanting to put the past behind us. But it would take a lot more than a few daiquiris and beads for me to forgive her.

"Oh my God I missed this," she said breathlessly. She placed a pair of beads around my neck and backed away as one of the high school bands started walking by. "Well, if you wouldn't have up and left us, then you wouldn't be missing this, now would you?"

"Seriously, Nia? Can we enjoy *one* outing without you ruining the moment?"

Was she serious?

"I'm not *ruining* anything! Nana may be able to just forgive you for what you did, Kissy, but I won't!" Kissy threw her hands up annoyed. "What is there to *forgive*, Nia? *Tell me what I did wrong?!*"

I could feel my blood boiling, but I refused to get loud right now. Even if the high school band was blaring their music next to us. "I won't sit here and entertain this conversation, Kissy! You *know* what you did! And on top of everything, you *took* money from Nana, and then just ran off like it was nothing!"

"It was an *investment*, Nia! One Nana understood, and one you haven't even asked me about!"

"*Because I don't care, Kissy!*" The crowd around us was starting to stare and the last thing I wanted to do was cause a scene. I stepped closer to her and lowered my voice. "Before you left, I kept mentioning over and over again, how badly I wanted to go to cosmetology school. Nana never *once* made an ounce of an effort to help me! Then here you go, mentioning a business idea down in Florida, and without hesitation, she ups and gives you twenty grand without blinking!"

Kissy pulled at her hair, looking distraught. "Nia, I really don't know *what* you want me to tell you. I'm sorry Nana didn't invest in your education, but it's not like I was standing in the way of it. All I want to do is be able to come home and be around my family without all *this*!"

I could tell she was being honest, and though there was a part of me that would've loved to bury the past, it was deeper than just some money. "Well, the fact is, you won't be here long so whether things are patched up between us or not, won't matter. You'll return to your perfect life in Florida, and I'll be here to take care of Nana till the old lady finally dies!"

I walked off, leaving Kissy standing there with a hurt look on her face. I was done talking, done bringing up the past, and overall, I was done with her! She'd find her own way home.

The bar was crowded and I knew it would be forever before I got a drink. I was reminded of another reason why I hated coming to New Orleans around Carnival season, but here I was, stuck in the middle of some packed bar on St. Charles.

"If *you* can't get a drink then I know I'm a lost cause!"

I turned around, shocked to see Greg standing in front of me. My anger soon vanished at the sight of his sexy ass. I could feel my entire body loosen up being so close to him. "What are you doing here?" I asked, not even trying to hide my excitement.

"Enjoying the parade with my wife and some friends. What are you doing here?"

"My sister's in town so we're spending some time together, catching up. I'm grabbing her a drink now," I lied convincingly.

"Why don't you guys join us? We're going to grab something to eat after this, then head over to my boy Keith's club that just opened!"

"*The Good Times Roll?* You *know* the owner?"

"Yea, we've been friends since college! You and your sister should come hang with us tonight!"

I felt tempted to say yes, but the idea of playing nice in front of Greg's wife was not my idea of a good time. That, and there was no way I could fake the funk being around Kissy right now. "Um, maybe some other time. It's been years since we've hung out so there's a lot to catch up on!" I could feel my body heat up as Greg smiled.

"You're so family orientated, that's what's up!

"What you getting, sweetheart," the bartender called out to me. "Please, let me get these for you. Can I get six daiquiris, please? Hypnotic and octane 190 mixed!" Greg ordered. I watched as he paid the bartender, then handed me two of them. "Tell your sister I said hi, and I'm glad she came around Carnival time. You ladies be careful, and enjoy yourselves!"

I watched as he quickly made his way through the crowd and out the door. An image of him and his wife snuggling together flashed through my mind and I couldn't help but feel a hint of jealousy. I handed the other daiquiri I was holding to some stranger in the bar and told him to enjoy. I had no intention of finding Kissy. I

needed to figure out a way to see Greg
again.

Greg

Keith grabbed the bar from out of my hands as I finished my last set. I was half shocked he had even showed up. I knew he was going to be busy since he opened the club, but weeks had gone by, and catching up with him was getting harder and harder. We always managed to at least work out together, but he had been skipping out on that as well.

"I was starting to think the only way I was going to see you again was through your social media or coming down to the club myself!" Keith laughed as we switched places. "Bruh shits been crazy hectic. I had to put out an ad for a club manager and promoter! Porsha is breathing down my back to hire a social media manager! Dude, doing everything *solo* is getting stressful." I waited until he knocked out his sets before finishing the conversation. I lifted the bar from his hands and set it back down.

"It's still early on in the game, everything will work itself out!" He wiped the bench off and we headed to the locker room. "Yea, I know. Just getting anxious, ya know. I thought the hard part was *opening* the club. Now I'm realizing I gotta work just as hard to keep it relevant."

I couldn't help but empathize with him. I remembered seeing my father spend many restless nights getting his practice to where it is now. One of the reasons I knew at a young age becoming a lawyer was my only option. I had to make sure his legacy carried on. Another reason I looked forward to having a baby. Though my child didn't have to be a lawyer, I wanted him, or her, to have something that would always belong to them.

"Well, you know if you need anything, I'm here for you." Keith dapped me off, "Definitely appreciate that. Make sure you and Mara make it the club one night soon! It'd be nice to see some familiar faces. You heading out?" he asked, walking out the locker room. "Nah, I'ma get a few more sets in before I head to work."

———————————

I dropped the dumbbells down and did a quick arm stretch. I had a ton of shit I needed to get done back at the office that I was avoiding. Since my dad had passed off some of his workload to me, I was determined to prove to him I deserved equal partnership in the company. I was calling it quits when I noticed a familiar face pop up behind me.

"Whoa, what are you doing here?" I asked.

Nia looked just as shocked as I was, walking up to embrace me, "You had completely sold me on this place the other night at the bar, saying how amazing of a gym it was. I thought I'd give it a try." I dodged her slowly, not wanting to get any of my sweat on her. "I've been here a while, you do not want to get this funk on any part of you, trust me."

I was surprised when she hugged me anyway. "Call me weird," she said pulling away, "but I enjoy the musk of a man. I find it to be sexy."

An awkward chuckle escaped my mouth. "Don't worry, I won't judge you." I ripped my workout gloves off and started heading to the locker room. "Well, it was good seeing you. I hope you enjoy the gym."

"Wait, Greg. I'd hate to be a nuisance, but the trainer doesn't come in for another hour. Any way you could show me how a few of these machines work?"

"Uh, yea, which ones did you have in mind?" I followed her to the glute machines, trying my best to keep my eyes off her butt as she sashayed in front of me. But I was the *only one* trying not to look. Every other man made it quite clear they enjoyed the view, and I couldn't lie, it was a sight to see. I could tell Nia was one of those women who knew she was sexy and had no issue carrying herself as such. Even with no makeup on, her face was unblemished, and she almost looked innocent. But I knew better.

There was a hint of a bad girl, hiding beneath the surface. It was a tad bit attractive.

I watched as she leaned over one of the machines, reading how to use it. "So, um, what exactly are you trying to work on?" I watched as she placed her hands on her hips. "I desperately want to tone down my hips. I feel like if they get any wider, I'll have to walk through doorways on an angle!" I laughed as I shook my head. "Nah, your hips are fine, Nia. Besides, you know New Orleans men like their women thick!"

"Clearly not, because my ass is single!"

I could only wonder what kind of men she had come in contact with that would not be interested in her. *Maybe she was crazy*, I thought. A stereotype attached to *many* light skin women from New Orleans. Especially the short ones.

"Why is it that you're single? If you don't mind me asking."

Nia gave me a clueless shrug. "I honestly *wish* I knew. There was this one guy I had been dating, and I just knew he was the one. Then the second he got a job opportunity out of state, he dropped my ass! I mean, I know I'm not perfect, and I have my share of flaws. But don't we all?"

"This is true. I think too often we try to find the perfect person, without realizing everyone is growing in their own way. You just have to find someone you're willing to grow with."

She gave me an intrigued smirk, "Is that how you and your wife ended up together? You knew she was someone you could grow with?"

"Quite the opposite, she was someone I wanted to grow *for*. Since college, she always seemed to have everything together, and it was the sexiest thing I had ever seen. I knew I had to be at my best to lock her down, and keep her."

"She's a lucky woman," Nia said, and I swore I could hear a hint of jealousy in her voice.

"And I'm a lucky man! But hey, when the right one comes along for you, you'll know. No need to rush it!" Nia just chuckled and added weights onto the machine. "That's the issue, whenever I think I've met the right one, there's always something wrong with them. Baby mama drama, their addicted to some kind of drugs, or. . ."

A look of unsureness came across her face and I could tell she was second guessing whether or not to finish her sentence. "Or what?" I probed.

"Or. . . they're married."

I cleared my throat and looked away, not trying to feel uncomfortable by the situation. I looked back as she was sitting down on the machine. She looked back at me and smiled, "Can you spot me?"

Shania

Nana and Kissy were sitting at the kitchen table when I walked in. I dropped my purse on the counter and folded my arms. It was clear they had been plotting something, so I was ready for an ambush. "Come sit down, Nia," Nana said, pushing a chair out for me. "I'll stand. I don't plan on being here long. I have a bar to open in a little while!"

"That's what we want to talk about, Nia. We both think it's a good idea for Kissy to start helping out since I can't be there like I used to." I laughed, "*Seriously*? That's your solution. Have Kissy work at the bar? Is that her way of making sure you leave her a portion of it in your will?"

"*Nia!*" Kissy snapped, but I refused to hear her excuses. "No, be honest! You want to make sure when Nana *dies* you at least inherit *something*, right? Is that why you came back? Your little business venture in Florida didn't work out?"

"On the contrary," Kissy snapped, "the *bar* I opened in Pensacola is a *success*! It's the reason I've been able to stay here and make sure Nana is ok. It's the reason I can *afford* to stay here and help *you*!"

A jolt of betrayal hit me. *A bar? She moved all the way to Florida to open a bar?* "Is that what you did with Nana's money? You blew it on a bar?"

"She didn't blow it, Nia," Nana said, finally speaking up. "I wanted her to invest somewhere else away from here in case things didn't work out in Chalmette with us buying the bar. I wanted you girls to have *something* you can call your own."

"So you sent *her*? You sent *Kissy* out into the world and kept *me behind* to babysit you?"

Nana had a wounded look on her face, but I didn't care. They could feed me whatever bullshit they wanted, but when it boiled down to it, Kissy was able to leave and explore the world, while I was stuck in Chalmette with this old lady. "Look, Nia, if it means that much to you, I'll stay in Chalmette and work at the bar. You can go to Florida and work there."

"You'd like that, wouldn't you? You both would *finally* be rid of me and can live your lives here without my bothersome ass around!"

"*Nia*," Nana called out distraught, "*what is it that you want, child?* You asked for help, Kissy is here! You hate Chalmette, she's giving you a way out!"

I snatched my purse up, prepared to head out the door. "Kissy can stay and help out with the bar, but I'm *not* going to Florida. I'll stay here and renovate the bar the way *I* want it to look. And once you *die*, Nana, I can sell this house and buy another bar in New Orleans that's truly *just* mine!" I walked out of the house not giving anyone the chance to say anything else to me. They had *always* made it clear that Kissy was the favorite. She always would be. I whipped my phone out my purse, shooting Greg a desperate text message.

"Please be free tonight! Family problems at home!"

I was more than glad Greg had suggested a night out. I was in desperate need of drinks, and fun! I was even more excited to finally be in The Good Times Roll. I had heard so much about this club, but since we pretty much had the same hours, coming to see it was impossible. Until now.

Maybe having Kissy around wasn't so bad, I thought slyly.

Greg was soon at my side handing me a shot. "To having a good night," he yelled to me. We tossed them down with ease, and he ordered four more from the bartender. "So, you wanna talk about what happened?" he asked. I reached for the shot as soon as the bartender set it down and gulped it down. "Nope," I said quickly, turning back to the crowd.

I could still feel the disappointment from the conversation earlier inside of me and I didn't want to lose control here. I wanted to have a good time tonight and I wasn't going to let Nana or Kissy ruin that for me.

The DJ began playing Juvenile's "Back That Azz Up," and all the ladies threw their hands up. Greg laughed as he looked around, "I am *convinced* this is every New Orleans girl's theme song!"

I grabbed his hand, trying to lead him to the dance floor. "Nah, that's. . . that's all you," he said timidly. I turned around slowly and did a quick booty shake for him. I could feel his eyes on me and desperately wanted to feel him behind me. I turned back to look at him, satisfied that his eyes were glued on my body. He tossed another shot back, making sure to stay away from me. I knew now was the only chance I would get to feel his body against mine, and I had to take it. I made my way back towards the bar to dance on him.

Before he could object, I immediately threw my ass against him, grinding extra hard. I could tell my moves were working. I could feel his hardness on my ass as I bent over and grinded up slowly. I whirled around and wrapped my hands around his neck. "You're trouble," he called out over the music. "You have no idea," I shot back at him. I wanted to take my chances and kiss him, but something else had caught his eye. "Hey, come with me to holla at my boy Keith!"

We exited off the elevator and I watched as Keith and Greg spoke. Another woman was sitting next to Keith in the VIP area, and I wasn't sure if we were interrupting something, but she, as well as Keith, looked uncomfortable when they saw me.

I watched as Keith and Greg walked over to the balcony, clearly arguing about something. After straining long enough to eavesdrop, I could tell it was about me. Clearly, Keith had an issue with Greg being here with someone who wasn't Greg's precious wife. I was gathering my purse as Greg walked towards me cursing.

"Dude doesn't even know what the fuck he's talking about!" He pushed aggressively on the elevator button till the doors closed. "Everything ok?" I asked, truly

worried. But Greg remained silent. I
decided not to say anything as we left out of
the club and got back into his car.

———————————

The ride back to my house was
awkwardly quiet, and Greg sat with a
disturbed look the entire time. "Want to
talk about it?" I asked, finally deciding to
break the silence. I could tell whatever
Keith said was bothering him. "This has
been my boy for *forever*, and instead of
coming to me man to man, he's gonna jump
to conclusions and assume I'm fucking
around with you!"

"So he thinks I'm some kind of side
chick?" I asked, doing my best to sound

insulted. Greg just shook his head. "Man, forget him and what he's talkin' bout! *I could care less.* You're too good to be a side chick for any man. I wouldn't do you like that!"

"Really?" I asked curiously, "how *would* you do me?" I could see a nervous look on his face and Greg began adjusting the temperature in the car. "Let me know if it gets too cold for you," he said casually. "The temperature's perfect for me."

Greg pulled into my driveway looking highly relieved. But I had no intention of letting him get out of this easily though. I had no idea when I would get another chance like this so I had to make it last.

"Sorry the night didn't go as planned," he apologized. "I would've never brought you there if I would've known it was going to go down like that."

I shook my head. "It's fine. I can understand how situations like this can look to other people. I'm just glad to know you had my back."

"Of course, you're an amazing woman, Nia. I wouldn't let anyone disrespect you like that."

I leaned forward so my body was closer to his. "Is that why you wouldn't do me like that? You wouldn't make me your side chick because you respect me too much?" I noticed his eyes glancing over my body, then back to his steering wheel. This was going to take a lot more effort than I thought. Hiking my dress up, I straddled him in his driver seat. Greg held his hands up quickly, caught off guard by my actions. "Nia, I. . ."

But I placed my index finger over his lips. "Shhhhh," I said, silencing him. "Please know," I said, placing kisses on his cheek, "I'd have enough respect to not only be your side chick but to keep everything that happens between us, between us."

I could feel his hardness against me, and before he had the chance to protest, I kissed him.

Mara

My eyes popped open as I heard the front door close. I glanced over at my alarm clock. Two thirty am. I listened as Greg fumbled up the stairs and into our bedroom. *Is he seriously drunk again?*

Our bathroom light came on and I turned over and watched him struggling to get undressed. Sighing, I tossed the covers back and headed into the bathroom to assist him. "Mara…Mara," he stuttered out. I could smell the alcohol on his breath as he rocked back and forth. "If Keith is going to have you coming home drunk like this, I'm going to have to ban you two from hanging out!"

"F-Fuck Keith!" Greg spat out, causing me to frown. I watched as he waddled over to the shower, his pants down to his ankles.

"Did you guys get into it?" I asked. It wasn't like the two of them to argue. The eight years I had known them, besides a few disagreements, I had never heard about them getting into it. Greg sat down and kicked his pants off. I watched as he climbed into the shower and sat down. I wanted to feel sorry for him, but this was one drunk night he'd have to deal with solo. I had a busy day tomorrow.

I chuckled as I watched him childishly try and bathe himself. Gathering his clothes, I headed downstairs to our laundry room. I couldn't wait to see how he would bounce back from this in the morning. I shook his pants to make sure there wasn't anything in his pockets before tossing them into the laundry basket. I was shaking his shirt out when I noticed stains on his collar.

I flipped the laundry room light on to get a better look. There was no denying the red stains were lipstick. Whoever it was for had kissed the collar almost perfectly. Almost intentionally. My chest began to tighten and I could feel my breath getting shorter and shorter as several scenarios ran through my mind. *Someone brushed against him*, I kept telling myself. *The club was packed and someone accidentally brushed against him.*

But my mind wouldn't let me be fooled. I balled the shirt up, wanting to storm back upstairs and confront him. I wanted to demand he explain to me what bitch got this close to him. *Relax, Mara, relax.*

Taking a deep breath in and out, I shoved the shirt to the bottom of the laundry basket and made my way back upstairs. Greg was already in the bed, passed out. I shoved him over to his side and climbed in, pulling the covers up to my neck. I looked back up at the clock. Not that it mattered, I wasn't going back to sleep anyway.

———————————

Porsha smiled when she walked into the restaurant to greet me. I stood up and kissed her on the cheek. "Thanks for meeting me, this couldn't wait!" Her smile disappeared when she saw the upset look on my face. "What happened?"

I yanked Greg's shirt out of my purse and dropped it on the table. It didn't take long for Porsha to notice what I had seen last night. *"Are you fucking serious?"* she hissed. *"Is Greg cheating on you?"*

Hearing the words out loud caused the tears I had been fighting to slide down my face. "Fuck," Porsha said, immediately coming to my side of the table to console me. "I'm. . . I'm ok," I choked out, wiping my tears away. "I don't have *real* evidence, just lipstick stains on his shirt!"

"Did you ask him about it?"

I shook my head. "If I confront him, and he tells me it's nothing, I'll want to believe him, Porsha! I need you to look into this for me?"

"You want me to *spy* on your husband?" she asked, and I could tell she was uncertain with the task I was giving her. "Not spy, just *investigate* him! There's no one else I can go to with this, Porsha. I *need* to know if there's someone else!" She took a deep breath and shook her head. "I've got a *bad* feeling about this, Mara. I cannot lie. As much as I am not a fan of Greg possibly cheating on you, catching him in action isn't going to make it any less painful for you!"

"You're absolutely right, but you finding everything out, will prevent him from being able to lie to me about!"

I could still tell Porsha was debating the idea back and forth in her head, and I was praying she would do this for me. She let out another huge sigh and said, "For *Greg's* sake, his ass better not be out here with some side bitch!"

Greg

I tapped my pen absentmindedly against my desk. I was supposed to be working, but Nia kept flashing in my mind. I replayed the other night over and over in my head, trying to figure out where I went wrong.

At one point in time did I give Nia the indication her kissing me was ok?

I avoided her since that night, clueless on what to say to make things go back to normal between us. She had sent an apologetic text to my phone the morning after, blaming her actions on the alcohol. But I knew it was no excuse. At least not on my end. I had brushed it off casually, trying to overlook that deep down inside, I wanted it.

I convinced myself if I kept it strictly professional between us, I could pretend as if nothing had happened. But here I was, sitting at my desk trying not to think about her. My phone vibrated, momentarily taking me out of my thoughts.

"I NEED to see you."

I held my breath as the text from Nia smacked me in the face. I could almost hear her saying the word "need" with eagerness. I shifted in my chair battling with the arousal trying to grow within me. *How was she able to seduce me with a simple text?*

"Got a moment?"

I looked up as my dad walked into my office. "Yes, of course," I said, quickly placing my phone face down. My dad sat down across from me and unbuttoned his jacket. I could see an uneasy look on his face and was worried that something was going on with the company. "Everything ok, Dad?"

"I just got off the phone with Mara, ya know, just checking in and seeing how she's been doing." I leaned forward as I pondered on what their conversation could have consisted of to make him so troubled. "She tells me you guys are going to need assistance from a doctor to have a baby."

Though the entire process had made me uneasy, hearing my father say it made me all of a sudden feel ashamed. Embarrassed. "Yes, a lot of couples turn to their doctors for help. It's becoming a common thing." But I wasn't sure if I was trying to convince him, or myself. My phone vibrated as a reminder that I had an unread message in my phone, but I ignored it.

"I don't know, son. There's something not right about a man needing help with making a baby. Are you sure everything is ok on your end?" I could feel the shame quickly turn into irritation and fought off the urge to tell him to get out of my office. "I'm fine, *Dad*, everything is fine! Mara and I are both two healthy adults. We're simply looking at other options in case they're needed!"

"It just seems strange, son, that's all I'm saying. I'm not sure how I'd feel about a test tube grandchild! What do I tell people when they ask how the child got here?"

"You don't tell them *anything*, Dad! It's no one's business how my son or daughter gets here! As long as they're here and loved!"

"Now wait just a minute," my dad said, tapping his finger on my desk. "What you do affects this company *and* our family. What would your mother think if she knew this is the route you all were taking to make a baby, Greg? It's not natural!"

My skin was on fire as I struggled to keep my composer. I could feel my entire body shaking as I reached for my buzzing cell phone. It was Nia calling. "Yes, Miss Comeaux. I received your message. I apologize for the delay. I'll be there in thirty." I hung up before Nia could speak, knowing quite sure that she was confused by my abruptness.

My father and I stood up and both headed towards my office door. "Sorry to rush you out, Dad, but duty calls." My father nodded understandingly as he buttoned his jacket back up. "Of course. I'm taking a few weeks off to visit your sister in Atlanta. If you need anything, contact Arthur. We will finish this discussion when I get back!"

I watched as Nia walked back from the kitchen carrying two glasses of wine. I was trying my best to stay focused, but the tight yoga pants she had on was very distracting. She handed me a glass as she sat down next to me smiling. "I *really* appreciate you driving all the way down here, Greg!" I set my glass down on the coffee table in front of the sofa. "You made it sound urgent, so I figured I'd come see what was going on. Is everything ok?"

Nia grabbed my glass and handed it back to me. "Everything's *perfect*! We're celebrating. The Comeauxs *officially* own Mama's Place! We finalized everything this morning!"

I couldn't help but smile and toasted with her. "Congratulations, Nia! I know how much this means to you and your family!" I watched as she downed her glass, then looked at me disapprovingly. "Why aren't you celebrating with me then?"

"It's, uh, it's a little too early for me to be drinking. I can take a rain check though." Nia placed her hand on my leg and pouted. "Aw, come on Greg, just *one* drink! Don't ruin this day for me!" Ignoring what my head was telling me, I took a small sip from my wine glass. "See, that wasn't so bad. Now let me show you the renovations I intend to make to the bar." I watched as she leaned forward and grabbed a small binder from the coffee table.

She scooted closer to me and I could smell her perfume. I struggled to keep my eyes on the photos she was showing me, but her breast sat up perfectly inside her spaghetti-strapped shirt, and it was as if they were eyeing me back. I reached for my wine glass and gulped the rest down. "Thirsty?" she asked. There was an amused look on her face and I wondered if part of her was enjoying this.

I sat the glass back down and stood up. "I should be heading back," I said, heading to her front door. She was up and right behind me, "Are you sure? You haven't even seen the rest of my pictures." I nodded and opened the door. "Yea, I have a meeting in an hour I need to prepare for. But I am happy for you and your family."

Nia wrapped both arms around me, "It was because of you, Greg. *All* of this happened, because of you!" Her hands slid slowly down my lower back and she pulled me in tighter. "Uh, Nia, I *need* to go!" She was shorter than me, but still managed to get on her tiptoes so her lips were damn near on mine. "Greg, do you *really* want to go?"

I paused before answering, and sensing this, she leaned forward and kissed me. A wave of regret hit me as soon as our lips touched, but I couldn't break away. The way our tongues intertwined was overwhelming and I felt a desire growing within me. Nia pulled away and slid her yoga pants down, and took her shirt off. She stood before me revealing her hourglass figure in a black strapless bra and matching thong. "I've been thinking about you fucking me since I met you," she admitted.

I watched as she seductively bit her lip and walked back towards the sofa. My mind was screaming for me to walk out the door. It was open and I was seconds away from my car. Nia made it to the sofa and turned back, fingering for me to come to her. With everything telling me otherwise, I found myself closing her front door, and locking it behind me.

———————————

The water wasn't hot enough for me to wash away the traces of Nia from off of my skin. I scrubbed violently, trying to wash her, and what I had just done, down the drain. But the more I scrubbed, the more intense each flashback became. My eyes closed and I could hear her moaning in my ear, begging me not to stop. I felt her soft ass bouncing back on me as I fucked her over her sofa. The look she gave me as she sucked me into an orgasmic state, swallowing every ounce of me. I could feel myself getting hard all over again and gave in to the urge to release the tension I was feeling.

"Need some help with that?"

I jumped at the sound of Mara's voice. She was standing outside of the shower, slowly undressing. Before I could speak, she was in the shower, placing kisses on my neck. Her hands replaced mine and I closed my eyes enjoying each stroke. Nia's body popped back into my head and I could taste her on my lips, the enthusiasm she had giving herself to me.

My eyes opened and Mara was kissing me, pushing her naked body against mine. I grabbed both her legs, wrapping them around me as I eased inside of her. Mara let a moan escape from her lips and whispered, "Make love to me, Greg, please."

My mind flashed back to Nia's legs wrapped around my neck just earlier. "*Fuck me, Greg, you better keep fucking me!*" she demanded. Mara's moans got louder and I could feel her body shaking in my arms. "Yes, Greg, oh my goodness, yes," she moaned.

"*Yes, Daddy! Oh yes,*" Nia moaned loudly. I remembered how she tightened her legs around me as she came, and I could feel Mara doing the same. As we climaxed together, I remembered the glow on Nia's face after she came. How relaxed and peaceful she looked as her body went limp.

Mara's hands were around my face and my eyes opened. "You ok?" she asked, breathlessly. I nodded persuasively, "Of course, baby. I'm fine!"

Shania

"Somebody got you glowing over there, Miss Nia!"

"Oh hush, Jeff!"

But I was quite aware that I *was* glowing. My mind constantly flashed back to yesterday and how amazing Greg was. I knew the very first time I laid eyes on him that man was going to be amazing in bed. And I *wasn't* wrong.

I hated how quickly he ran out of the house after we were done, but I'm sure he had to run back to wifey! I could feel my mood dampen as the idea of him fucking me, then snuggling with her came into my mind. I shook my head so the image would escape from my thoughts. I knew what I was getting myself into when I made up my mind to seduce Greg. But now that I had a sample of him, I would be damned if I was going to *just* be a side chick.

The bar door swung open and I watched as my sister walked in. "Whoa, whoa, whoa!" I heard Jeff call out. Kissy smiled as she embraced him. "Hey, Jeff. How are you?"

"Great, now that you're here! Was starting to think you had completely disappeared on us! I almost forgot what you *looked* like!"

I watched as both of them laughed and Jeff's stupid joke and realized my happy moment wasn't going to last long. "What do you want, Kissy?"

She made her way to the bar and sat across from me. "I just left Nana's follow up appointment. They want to do triple bypass surgery on her, Nia."

I immediately got aggravated with the concerned look on her face. "*And?*"

"Nia, *seriously?* At Nana's *age*, that could be dangerous! Aren't you the least bit scared of losing her?"

I laughed as I continued to wipe down the bar. "She'd be doing me a favor if she died, *trust me!*"

"Nia, stop being a bitch for two seconds please! This is serious!"

"*I am being serious, Kissy.* Nana is barely on her last leg and she needs to let that go. You get to sit here and be concerned about her surgery because you're not the one who has to pay for it! I am!"

"Nia, I can help pay for the surgery, it's not about the money, and you know it!"

I tossed the towel at her face and walked from behind the bar. "You can feed Nana whatever bullshit you want, Kissy. But since you volunteered to stay, you open the bar. I have an errand to run," I lied. Truth was, I couldn't stand being around her longer than five minutes without them reminding me of how much of a disappointment I was.

I was halfway to my car when to my surprise, I saw Greg's car pull up. I was excited at first, as he got out and made his way towards me. Then I realized the upset look on his face. "We need to talk." I looked back at the bar. There was *no way* he was going to meet Kissy's ass.

"Let's talk in your car."

I had never been more grateful for tinted windows as I locked myself inside of Greg's car. He was barely making eye contact with me as he stared out his window. "Nia, *I cannot* do this," he stated firmly.

"Do what, Greg?"

"*I cannot cheat on my wife!* I *will not* cheat on my wife!"

Newsflash, you're a little too late for that one, I thought. But I could hear the regret and anger inside his voice. "Um, Greg, I really don't know what you want me to say. I enjoyed our time together yesterday, and I thought you did too."

I waited for him to smile, to brag on how great the sex was between us. But he remained silent as he continued to stare out the window.

Oh, this dude feels guilty-guilty!

I knew Greg was a decent man, but I had no idea he would feel this bad behind what we did. I knew *plenty* of men who cheated and felt fine after. But not Greg. His guilt showed all over his face. His pain. His regret. I quickly straddle him in his driver seat and brought my face close to his. "Greg, you *didn't do* anything wrong." I began placing kisses on his face and down his neck. "You got caught up in a moment that no one has to know about, but me and you!"

Greg still refused to look at me, even with my face within kissing distance from his. "Nia, you seriously don't understand. I am not this type of man. *I love my wife!*"

"And no one's asking you to stop! Everything in life happens for a reason. *This* happened for a reason. And I don't feel bad about figuring out why!"

Damn, I'm good!

I had to pat myself on the back. I could tell Greg was believing the bull I was dishing out. Hell, I was starting to believe it myself!

Truth is, *I wanted him*, and I was *going* to have him! His eyes avoided me at all costs, but I could tell my presence was affecting him. The hardness growing in between his legs let me know I had his attention. I reached over at the lever on the side of his seat and pulled it up so his seat reclined back. "Nia . . . Nia, I *need* you to stop," he pleaded.

But I was already on the floor in front of him, unzipping his pants. His voice kept begging for me to stop, but the way he responded as I proceeded to go down on him, let me know he truly meant otherwise.

Mara

The look on Porsha's face when I opened my front door, shattered any hopes I had of my suspicions being wrong. *Greg was cheating*, I could see it all over her face. "Mara," she started to say, but even she didn't have the heart to say it out loud.

I could feel my heart pounding in my chest and I reached for the wall to catch my balance. There was a pain I had never felt before and I was convinced I was having a heart attack. Clutching my chest, I allowed my legs to give as I collapsed to the floor. Porsha rushed in and scooped me in her arms. I don't know when I started crying, but I could hear myself hysterically sobbing in her arms as she rocked me.

Images of Greg and I flashed quickly through my mind. The day we met our first kiss, the first time we made love. . . *our wedding*. My mind began racing with thoughts of, *It's a lie! She's wrong, Porsha is wrong! She's never liked Greg, why not lie to me?*

But I knew better.

My heart knew better. Porsha would rather bite her arm off than lie to me about something like this. I took deep breaths in, trying to calm myself down before I had a panic attack. Porsha leaned back to look at me and I realized she was crying as well. Hatred began to grow inside of me at that moment. A hatred I had no idea I was capable of feeling. *Ever.*

"Who-who is she?" I managed to choke out. "Is she *anyone* we know?" Porsha shook her head. "No, never seen the woman a day in my life, honestly. I believe she's one of his dad's clients. They met maybe over a month ago, but it was *just* business. I'm not sure when it became more than that, but it has."

A million thoughts ran through my mind as I recalled every single "business meeting" he had been claiming he was going to. And all his late nights at the office. Was all of that a lie? Was it all a cover-up so he could be with whoever this woman was? "Where does she work?"

"Some bar in Chalmette," Porsha said. She watched as I finally stood up and wiped my tears away. I grabbed my keys off the key hook that hung by the door and turned back to her.

"Let's go see this bitch!"

———————————————

I felt ridiculous entering into the bar wearing a blonde wig Porsha *conveniently* had in her car. I had side-eyed her when she tossed it to me, wondering what kind of kinky things she was into. She sucked her teeth when she noticed my questioning stare. "It's for when I'm investigating a story, geesh!"

She helped me pull my hair back and secure the wig in place. "Here," she said, handing me a pair of shades, "just in case this bitch knows what you look like!"

I felt an ache inside my chest. "How would she *know* that?"

"Name *one* movie you've ever seen where the mistress *didn't* know what the wife looked like? *They have to know!* Well, if they're smart they would *want* to know what she looks like! You don't want to have some random woman whippin' your ass and you have no idea why!" I hated that as upset as I was, her words made me laugh. We got out of the car and headed into the bar.

It was crowded when we walked in, and I was grateful that we would be able to go unnoticed. Porsha pointed to a seat at the back facing the bar and keeping my head down, I made my way there, while she went to the bar to get our drinks.

I sat down and watched as she chatted with the lady behind the counter. A minute later, she was sliding in the seat next to me with two beers. "*That's her,*" she whispered, though she did not need to.

My heart broke again as I looked up at the woman fooling around with my husband. I wanted her to be ugly, with bad weave, crooked teeth, and a flat ass. I wanted her to be hideous, so I could convince myself that Greg had lost his *entire* mind and that's the only reason he would cheat on me. But the universe wasn't that kind.

She was beautiful, and it pained me to admit it. She was a smidge shorter than me, light skin, natural hair, and thick, just how Greg liked his women. I hadn't even touched my beer but felt the urge to throw up. "You wanna confront her? Cause we can, I'm totally ok with checking this bitch!" Porsha said quickly. A vision of her smashing her beer bottle on the table and confronting the woman flashed in my mind, and I was a little ashamed by the comfort it brought me. "No," I said, not wanting to cause any kind of scene here. "I just want to go."

Porsha gave me an understanding nod, and we stood up to leave. We were seconds away from the door when it swung open and Greg walked in. Faster than I knew a human being was capable of moving, Porsha grabbed me and snatched me down into a booth. My heart was beating rapidly in my chest and I couldn't figure out why *I* was currently scared of getting caught here.

Porsha pulled her hood over her head and turned to face the window so he wouldn't recognize her either. "*He's supposed to be at work!*" I whispered angrily.

We both watched, undetected, as he walked over to the bar. The lady behind the bar's eyes lit up and she leaned forward to hug him. I watched in disgust as they kissed right there in front of *everyone*!

So, he's public with this hoe?

My stomach was churning and whatever was going to come up wasn't going to stay down long. We watched as she guided him to what we could only assume was a back office and closed the door. Porsha and I simultaneously jumped up and raced towards the back where my car was parked. As soon as I knew we were in the clear, I leaned over and threw everything I had been trying to contain up.

Greg

I reached for my phone on the nightstand as my alarm started to go off. It wasn't needed since I had yet to go to sleep. The guilt from my actions was constantly haunting me every time I attempted to close my eyes. Even holding Mara brought me no kind of relief. I had found myself staring at her while she slept. How peaceful she looked. How at that moment, she had nothing in the world to worry about.

I could feel the anxiety swell inside of me as I realized how my actions would quickly take that peace of mind away if she were to ever find out about Nia.

She could *never* find out.

Conversations replayed back and forth in my head throughout the night of ending things with Nia, but something kept holding me back. My eyes popped open and I stared at the ceiling as if it contained the answers I needed. As long as I had known Mara, there was no other woman I had ever wanted. She was everything I needed.

But there was something about Nia, something I couldn't put my finger on that was driving my crazy.

My second alarm went off and I knew now it was time to get out of the bed.

My sister's face suddenly appeared on my screen. "Sup, Ash?"

"I hate when you call me that," she shoot back. I couldn't help but chuckle at the slightly annoyed sound in her voice. "Sorry, old habits die hard!"

"Uh-huh," she said, unconvincingly. "I'm in town and stopped at the house and was trying to see why Dad hasn't been checking his mailbox. Is he going to be at work today?"

"Uh, Ashley, Dad's supposed to be in Atlanta with you," I reminded her, starting to feel apprehensive. My dad was still in good shape, so there was no need to fear for his safety if he was out there alone. But I wasn't a fan of Ashley not remembering that. "No," she finally said, "I got a text him from his last week canceling those plans. Something about working a case with you the next few weeks and he couldn't make it!"

It didn't take long for my sister to figure out my father was lying to one of us and start to imagine the worse. "Greg, is Dad ok? Is something wrong with him?"

Her tension was making its way through the phone and I know I would have to remain calm for the both of us. I forced a laugh out of my mouth, "Dad probably found himself a new boo and didn't want to tell us! He's fine! I'll catch up with Arthur today and get the scoop on everything."

I could hear her breathing return to normal, but now the question of where my dad *really* was, was lingering on my mind.

Mara was on her computer, focused on some new merchandise she had received. "Good morning," I said, walking into her office. I placed a kiss on her forehead, but she never stopped typing. "Morning," she muttered out.

"Article that intense, huh?" I teased her.

"Yea, sorry," she replied dryly. I could feel the guilt rising inside of me as my conscience began whispering to me she was upset.

She knows!

But I pushed the thought out of my head. I knew Mara, there was no way she knew.

"Anything you want to do this weekend?" I asked, determined to have some kind of friendly conversation with my wife before I left. Even if it was to ease the regret I was feeling. "I have plans with my mother this weekend. I'll let you know if anything changes."

I had wanted to mention the phone call with Ashley to her, to see if I could get *some* kind of emotional response from her. But I decided to just leave her be. "Well, I'll be home a little after six tonight, but call me if you need *anything!*" I assured her. I kissed her lovingly on top of her head before heading out. I looked back one last time to see if she would at least say, "I love you." But she never once looked up.

I took a deep breath as I knocked on his office door.

"Come in."

I wasn't surprised at all when I saw Keith's reaction when I walked in. He dropped the pen he was holding down and leaned back in his chair. "Can we talk?" I asked.

We hadn't spoken since he blew up on me at the club weeks ago, and though I know I wasn't getting any sympathy from him, I needed someone to talk to.

"I'm listening," Keith said coolly. I walked in and closed the door behind me. Taking a seat across from him, I know it made no sense to beat around the bush.

"Man, I didn't mean to bring any nonsense to your club. I honestly wasn't thinking about it at the time. Like in my head, she was having a rough night, and I just wanted her to have fun. I never thought about the predicament it would put you in."

Keith just continued to stare at me, and I couldn't tell whether he was accepting my apology or not. He finally leaned forward and said, "Are you sleeping with her?"

I knew the question was unavoidable. And honestly, it was one of the reasons I was here. I *needed* someone to talk to. My silence was all Keith needed as he jumped out of his chair. "*Damnit, Greg. Are you fucking serious?*"

"Bruh, I don't know what happened. Like one minute I was thinking we were just friends, and then the next. . ."

"Man, miss me with the '*oops I slipped in it*' story. You fucked that climber because you wanted to." As bad as I felt, I wasn't going to let him talk about Nia like that. "Keith, the girl isn't a climber. She has her own bar now, she's making her own money. She doesn't *need* me to get her anywhere in life!"

Keith just shook his head. "Man, I'm trying with everything in me not to call this female out her name, but that *hoe* is a *climber*! It's all on her face! In her demeanor! You just too busy in her ass to see it!"

I never expected Keith to have sympathy for Nia, but hearing him continue to bash her made me realize coming here might not have been a good idea. "Did you at least use protection?" he asked, hopelessly.

"No, son, I didn't! And spare me the lecture of *that* as well!"

I stood up and headed for his office door. I knew I was wrong, and already felt an ocean of guilt. The last thing I needed was someone else making me feel worse.

I heard Keith push his chair back as he was following right behind me. "Greg, sit your ass down!" he demanded. I felt myself freeze as my hand was on the knob. I could hear the anger, and the hurt, in his voice.

"You came here to talk, now we're talking!" Keith said. I let go of the doorknob and turned around to face him. "What do you want me to say, huh? I *know* I fucked up, and I know the risk I just took. *I have no idea how to fix this shit!*" I confessed to him.

Keith let out a helpless sigh and made his way to a small fridge in his office. He took out two beers and handed me one. "Does Mara know yet?" he asked. I shook my head as I gulped down half my beer.

"Do you *want* to be married?"

I had played around with that question every time I was on my way to see Nia. The closer I would get to her, the more guilt I would feel. But as soon as I saw her, it was like nothing mattered but just the two of us at that moment. And the second I stepped away from her, that guilt was right back at it, eating me alive. I could feel myself becoming distant from Mara, not wanting her to touch me, fearing she'd be able to sense I had been with someone else. I knew there would come a day she would mention the distance between us and I had no idea how I was going to handle that.

"I love Mara more than anything, Keith. I don't know what I'm going to do."

Keith placed a reassuring hand on my shoulder. "*First*, you're going to get tested to make sure that climber didn't give you shit. Then you're going to do some serious praying that she didn't!" As serious as he was being, we both laughed together.

"And then?" I asked, genuinely needing guidance. "Then you're going to cut all ties with this chick, and come clean with your wife!"

It was words I hadn't wanted to hear, but I knew it was the truth. There was no way I was going to be able to continue in my marriage without coming clean. All I could do was pray that when Mara found out the truth, she would love me enough to stay.

Mara

She floated back and forth with such ease, speaking to the men sitting around the bar. I watched as she gave them affectionate looks, and winks, and wondered if that's how she had hooked my husband. I had always thought he was a stronger man than that. Too strong to be tricked by some tight jean wearing, cleavage showing woman. But clearly, he was just a man. I leaned forward rubbing at my temples. Porsha's wig was starting to give me a headache, but I had no choice but to wear it. I couldn't take the chance of her recognizing me.

The idea of her even *knowing* what I might look like continued to concern me. *Was he showing her pictures of me? Did they sit around critiquing how I looked?*

Maybe he hadn't told her about me! Maybe I was some secret and he was ashamed of me!

I pulled at the jacket I was wearing, slowly becoming self-conscious. I had always been confident, not conceited, just confident. One of the things Greg *claimed* made him fall in love with me. Even after gaining a little weight I still felt sexy, and he had never complained. *Maybe he's complaining to her*, my mind taunted me. I shoved the table away and stood up. I had tortured myself long enough studying this woman. It was clear her looks caught his attention, and I'd never know what else piqued his curiosity.

My body froze as I realized she was walking towards me, smiling. "Now, you've been here almost every day this week, sitting over here in this corner, babysitting one beer for hours! Either you're not a real drinker, or you're plotting a murder," she teased.

You have no idea.

"Um, I was just debating on what I wanted," I lied.

"*For a week*? There are not that many alcohol choices in the world! Follow me to the bar, I'll make you something special!"

Against my better judgment, I followed. "That's your last one, Joe, you hear me? Your wife's not gonna call down here fussing at me because you're not home in thirty minutes!" I couldn't resist the urge to laugh.

At least she has concerns for somebody's wife. Just clearly not my husband's!

I sat down on the barstool in front of her as I watched her prepare some kind of concoction with tequila in it. I usually preferred vodka, but figured, *why not*!

She slid the drink towards me and leaned forward, a smile never leaving her face. Her hazel eyes appeared to be sizing me up and I pushed my glasses back, scared she was beginning to recognize who I was. "Well?" she asked as I took the first sip.

"It's good," I muttered out, downplaying how great the drink was. *Was that it? Did you get him drunk? Is that how it all started?*

I never took my eyes off of her as I downed the rest of the drink, then slammed the glass on the bar. She nodded with an impressed smile on her face. "A woman who can hold her liquor. *I like that*!" She gave me a wink as she proceeded to make me another one. I pulled my jacket off as she slid the drink to me. "Only if you drink with me," I challenged. She quickly made a drink of her own and raised it to me. "Cheers."

Our glasses clinked and I gulped down half of my second drink, while she completely downed hers. "Alright now, *Miss Nia*," one of the men called out to her. I watched as she wiped her mouth and flipped him off. "I see you got jokes, Jeff. *Don't play with me!*"

I leaned forward, "Nia, is it?"

"Uh, yea, yea it's Nia," she said, still smiling. I leaned back and finished off my second drink. "Nice to meet you."

I watched as she continued to ramble on about something I had stopped listening to minutes ago. But clearly my face showed interest because she never stopped talking. I could see why Greg was into her. She was an entertainer. She had everyone in the bar mesmerized by her. The men laughed when they were supposed to and commented when needed. I found myself getting lost in her a few times and had to remember why I was here.

"Are you ok? Are you going to need me to call you a cab?"

I blinked quickly, refocusing my vision as I realized she was staring at me. I looked around and realized everyone else had gone. "No, no, I'm fine. I'd better be leaving."

I slipped my jacket back on and reached for my wallet. "What's the damage?" But she shook her head, "It's on me," she said smoothly. I could feel the frown form on my face. "But I can *pay* for this!" I could only wonder what I looked like to this woman. She was probably starting to think I was homeless. Sweatpants, a huge t-shirt with a too-big jacket on. And let's not forget the crazy blonde wig!

I watched as she waved her hand, "It's *really* not necessary. You looked like you had a lot on your mind, I just wanted to help."

I don't know if it was the alcohol, or me having enough of this good girl image she was portraying, but a laugh escaped my lips, and I could see the confusion on her face. "How could *you* possibly help me, huh? *How?*"

"Is there something you want to talk about?" she asked, concerned. Or it could've been fear on her face. I couldn't tell. I could only feel a wave of fury rushing through me.

"Talking won't help! Talking *never* helps! All it does it make you face what's wrong and how *fucked up* people really are!" The tears were burning at my eyes, but I refused to let her see them. I could feel myself making a fool of myself right now, and wanted nothing more but to disappear from her sight.

I watched as she walked around the bar to face me. *Shit*, I thought. I wasn't drunk, but not sober enough to fight. I mentally kicked myself wishing I would've taken Porsha's advice and never came back here. I watched as she reached for my face and I quickly blocked her. "Relax," she said gently, taking a step towards me. Her vibe radiated an emotion of calmness that I could feel hit me. She reached for my face again and slowly pulled my shades of.

I looked at her confused as she began to smile. "There you are," she breathed out. I could feel my body tense up as she leaned in closer. I felt paralyzed all over as I felt her hands around my face. Her eyes went from my eyes to my lips, and just as I was realizing what was happening, she kissed me.

The sun was making its way through the balcony blinds, but I wasn't ready to wake up. I wasn't ready to face today. My mind replayed last night over and over in my head and I couldn't shake the memory of Nia's lips on mine. I felt myself tracing the outline of my lips, reminiscing on how soft and intense the kiss had been. How I could feel myself wanting more, and how I had to fight myself to break away. I remembered the confusion in her eyes as I started crying and stormed out.

It was clear she didn't know who I was. There's no way she would've kissed me if she did. Or maybe she did, and this was some sick, twisted game she and Greg were playing. I could feel a headache forming as hundreds of questions and scenarios flooded my mind. I needed to get to the bottom of this. I *needed* answers. I tossed my covers back and hopped out of the bed.

I watched her pull up and park her truck next to mine. There was a semi-shocked look on her face as she hopped out and made her way over to me. There was a look in her eyes that I couldn't figure out. A look that made *me* feel guilty for how I reacted last night. "Hey, I wasn't sure I'd see you again," she admitted.

"I hadn't planned on it myself," I confessed.

I tried to form words in my head that made sense. I was a ball of emotions and all I wanted to do was scream.

"*Why did you kiss me?*" I demanded.

"I'm sorry, I *really* am! I had *no idea* why I did it, I'm not even sure if you're into women. I just saw you, looking so distraught behind *something*. Like you were lost. Last night you just looked like you needed something, and I couldn't resist the urge to kiss you!"

I frowned as I listened to her almost convincing confession. I held my left hand up, "I'm *married*, Nia!"

A horrified look spread across her face, "I'm...I'm *so* sorry. I didn't mean to...*I didn't know*!"

Somebody get this bitch an Oscar!

She could tell I was unmoved by her words and began backing up. "Look, I'm not the type to just kiss random women, especially married ones! So, again, I apologize. I hope whatever you're battling with gets better!"

"*It's my marriage!*" I found myself yelling out to her. Maybe if she knew, maybe if she *understood*, she'd leave my husband alone. I watched as she paused, clearly debating what to say next. "Do you want to come inside and talk about it?" she asked, hope in her voice.

A wave of confusion swept over me as my body followed her inside. She pulled two bar stools down and sat down beside me. "I like the brown, by the way," she said, commenting on the fact I wasn't wearing my wig today. I had stormed out the house with one goal in mind I had completely forgotten to grab it. I ran my fingers through my loose curls and nodded. "Yea, this is me."

She smiled and reached forward, twisting her finger around one of my curls. The look in her eyes was as if she was trying to read my thoughts. "Talk to me," she said softly. I swallowed the knot forming in my throat. What was I supposed to say? Tell her the truth, that I know who she was and that she's sleeping with my husband? Or play at this game she was so good at.

A vindictive side came over me and I realized I wanted to play.

"It's just problems at home. My husband's staying out late, drinking more, becoming distant. I don't know what to do." Nia took a deep breath in. "You don't think he's cheating, *do you?*"

Yes, bitch, with your hoe ass!

I shrugged convincingly. "I honestly don't know! He's never given me reasons to think he would. And I can't imagine *any woman* wanting to sleep with a married man!"

"You'd be surprised! Some women just don't care. They actually prefer married men!"

Like your hoe ass, huh?

"Have you tried talking to him?"

I shook my head. "I wanted to gather all my information first. Do some investigating, see what I can find."

"Oh, that's not a good idea," she said, critically.

Bitch, I know you lying!

I stood up realizing I couldn't handle this anymore. She was up with me as I headed to the door. Her hand was over the door, blocking me from opening it. "Look, I didn't mean to upset you, I just don't think snooping is the best thing. Talk to your husband. Ask him *directly*! If he lies, *then* investigate. But at least give him a chance!"

"Why are you on his side? Why do you feel like he'll do the honorable thing and come clean?"

It's because you're fucking him, isn't it?

Nia moved her hand off the door. "I want to believe he'd do right by you. I've known you less than twenty-four hours, and *I* already want to do right by you!"

An unfamiliar sensation shot through me as I realized she was possibly coming on to me. I shook my head and grabbed the door. Her hand was on my arm, whirling me around.

There was a look in her eyes that was captivating to me. I could feel everything in me wanting to run out the door. But the look on her face was convincing me to stay. Realizing I was no longer in a hurry to rush out, she smiled at me. "I'm not in the habit of kissing women whose name's I don't even know."

"I'm. . . I'm Mara."

Shania

I stared at the screen of my phone, waiting. I had texted Greg over an hour ago and still nothing. And when I called, I was getting his voicemail. There was a huge part of me trying not to overreact, but it was clear, he was trying to pull away.

Even our last conversation made it obvious he was brushing me off. I could remember how he kept stuttering up excuses about why he couldn't come to my house that night.

"My wife. . . my wife isn't feeling good, Nia. I tried meeting you for lunch but you were busy!"

"I had plans for lunch, Greg, which is why I'm trying to see you now!" I was high key annoyed, but arguing with him wouldn't get him here. Only give him a reason to stay away. I could hear the noise in the background and I knew he was in the car. "Look, I won't keep you long, baby. I promise. I just miss your hands all over me," I said seductively.

He was silent, and I knew he was thinking about it. I was just about to get up and shower, when he said, "I'm sorry, Nia. I can't," and hung up before I could protest.

That was three days ago. I glanced back down at my phone. Still nothing. Aggravated, I tossed my phone onto my bed and stormed into the kitchen. I was more than sure he was going back on one of his guilt binges, and it was becoming more and more tiresome. Every time he left me, I had to spend the entire next day soothing him, letting him know he wasn't a bad person for cheating on his *beloved* wife. And it was starting to get old.

An unexpected knock pulled me out of my thoughts. It was too early to be Greg, even though my body was hoping it was. I checked my reflection in my hallway mirror before swinging my front door open.

"Can we talk?"

"*Why the fuck are you here, Kissy?*"

My sister stared back at me, and I knew she wasn't going to speak until I let her in. I pushed the door open so she could walk in.

She sat down on my sofa and began fidgeting with her finger. "What do you want?" I asked again. This wasn't a pleasant surprise, so I wasn't going to act like it. "I've been talking to Nana, and I think after she has the surgery, she should move down to Florida with me."

"*Fuck you!*" I lashed out. Her face looked offended, but I didn't buy into it for one minute. "Nana is going to stay here, *with me*. The person who's *been* taking care of her!"

"Nia, you make Nana feel like she's a burden to you! Why keep her here?"

"She *is* a burden, Kissy! She's *my* burden, and I'm not going to let you take her down to Florida away from me!"

I could tell my sister was confused, and I never expected her to understand. Of course, she wanted Nana around her. She wanted to make amends for what she had done, for ruining our lives! For ruining Nana's life! But I wasn't going to let that happen. I was *never* going to allow her to make peace with what she had done! Wasn't going to happen.

"The reality of it is its Nana's choice. If she *wants* to leave, she can!" Kissy challenged me.

"*I dare you and Nana to try me!* I have a lawyer in my back pocket who I'll convince to say otherwise. I'll prove Nana is unfit to make any kind of decisions. Not only will she stay here, but I'll also make sure I gain *complete* control of the bar!" I had no clue if any of what I was saying was possible! But, fortunately for me, my sister was just as ignorant of the legality of things as I was.

"I have *no idea* why you hate me and Nana so much, Nia. But I seriously hope you let it go! You'll never be happy!"

I laughed at her advice. "You and Nana are the ones who will have to accept what you guys have done, not me!" I could tell my sister wanted to say more, but there was nothing left to discuss. "You can leave now, Kissy!"

She stood up to make her way to the door and began to sway a bit. "Why's it so hot in here?" she asked, fanning herself.

"It's seventy-one degrees, Kissy. What are you talking about?"

Her face began to go pale as if she had seen a ghost. "Are you going to throw up?" I asked, racing to my front door. "I just need some air," she said, trudging out my house. She turned back to me, clutching her stomach. "Just think about it, Nia, please."

Not giving her any hope, I slammed the door behind her. She and Nana were both losing their minds if they thought it was something I would consider. I made way to my bathroom to grab some Lysol. I don't know what had taken over her, but if she had some kind of stomach bug, I didn't want to catch it.

The conversation replayed in my mind, and I couldn't help but wonder how the conversation at Nana's went. Had they been excited at the idea of leaving me behind? Had Nana hated me that much that she would leave me here alone?

I could feel the hurt boiling inside of me. Kissy, no matter what, would be Nana's favorite. After *everything* she had put us through, Kissy would always be better than me!

As I stood up from grabbing the can, I immediately felt dizzy. I began fanning myself as my skin was getting hot. *Had I gotten sick that quick?*

Before I could answer myself, my head was in the toilet, and I was throwing up everything I had eaten that day.

Mara

My hands tapped anxiously on the table, even though at this point, I had no reason to be nervous anymore. But after two weeks, I still was. And no matter how many times I convinced myself she was a regular person, just like me, I wasn't buying it.

There was just *something* about being around Nia that put me on edge. Originally, I blamed it on her figuring out who I was and calling me out. But after we exchanged numbers at the bar, and started hanging out, it was clear she didn't know I was Greg's wife. And I made quite sure to *never* mention his name around her.

Though my intentions with her were still the same, the naïve side of me believed an actual friendship was forming. She had made an appoint to text me every day, just to check in and make sure I was ok. She would find random reasons to text me throughout the day, and there was a small part of me that looked forward to seeing her number pop up on my screen. There were times Greg would be sound asleep, and she and I would be up having some in-depth conversation, which weirdly enough, brought me some kind of amusement.

I smiled when she walked through the door and headed towards my table. "Hey beautiful," she greeted me as we embraced. "Was the place hard to find?" she asked, sitting down across from me.

"Not really, I just never heard of this place before. That, and I tried to avoid Magazine Street. The traffic is so hectic!" I admitted to her. "True, but this place has the best lemon drop martinis, and the best sushi, I *promise*!"

I watched as her hazel eyes scanned through the menu. She always had this look of enthusiasm, which despite how I knew her, made me want to think she wasn't a bad person.

"So, how are things on your end?" she asked.

"Business is going good," I responded, trying to sound vague. I lied and told her I was a brand ambassador for an upcoming business whose name I couldn't reveal just yet. The last thing I needed was for her to Google me and see who I was.

"I can't *wait* for them to finally launch so you don't have to be so secretive all the time! The job sounds thrilling!"

"One day, soon, it'll all be revealed." I could feel an eerie feeling come over me. This would end soon. These lunch dates, the texting, the motivational conversations. The relationship with Nia all together would end soon, and it was something that poked at me whenever I realized how happy I was around her. The truth would come out one day, and what would happen to our friendship then?

I could feel my chest began to tighten and reached for my glass of water. "How's...how's the bar," I asked, trying to sound interested. Nia took in a deep breath. "Can we talk about *anything* else?" And I knew she was avoiding the topic of her sister. "Still that bad, huh?"

"Let's just say we're starting the renovations and I'd rather be outside in the sun building the bar from scratch than listen to her bark out orders."

"And your Nana?"

Nia's face lit up. "She's doing great! The surgery went *amazing*! I cannot wait to get her home! I really can't wait for her to see the bar once it's finished!"

I couldn't help but smile at the closeness she had with her grandmother. Both of my grandparents passed while I was still young, and though I had a great relationship with my parents, I longed to know the people who raised them. "Your grandmother is very lucky to have you around!"

"Yea, that's what they tell me!"

The waiter finally came and took our order. I sat back and watched as Nia ordered everything she wanted me to try. And since sushi was her area of expertise, I didn't object. Once he left, Nia turned her attention back to me.

"But how are your matters of the heart?"

"My marriage?" I asked, knowing it was a conversation I didn't want to discuss. She would try and bring it up randomly and I would do my best to divert the dialogue elsewhere. But seeing as in how our first encounter was me pretty much breaking down behind my husband, I was sure that would always be something she was curious about.

"Everything's fine, we're taking things one step at a time," I lied. "So, did you find out whether or not it was another woman?" she pressed.

The uneasiness caused me to shift in my chair, and I knew my body language was obvious to her. We were both relieved when the waiter brought us our drinks. Without waiting, I instantly gulped mine down. "You're right, they are good here!"

Nia continued to drink hers down, nodding in agreement. "And the best thing about it is, it's *happy hour*!"

I walked alongside her as we made our way passed the shops on Magazine Street. She was obsessed with the clothing stores for some strange reason and had talked me into tagging along with her. "Here we are," she said, finally pulling me into a store with some vintage, but cute, clothes.

I followed closely by while she flipped through the racks, grabbing what she liked. "You know what I realize, you *never* mention a boyfriend," I said, waiting for her reaction. Nia laughed as she held a dress up. "I thought I gave off the impression that men weren't my thing."

"So you're gay?"

Maybe that was it. Maybe she and Greg had some kind of freaky group sex relationship going on that he knew I wouldn't be into. *Was my husband some kind of sex freak that I didn't know about?*

I followed Nia as she made her way to the dressing room. "Um, as cliché as this sounds, I *really* hate labels. Have I dated men? Yes. Do I date women? Yes!"

"So you're bi?" I continued to push. I
waited for her to lash out an annoyed
response, but she remained cool. "Let's just
say, I like what I like. If I'm attracted to
you, mentally, physically, and emotionally,
I'm going to date you!"

Her words made me think back to the
night she kissed me, and I felt myself
touching my lips. "Did you think I was gay
the night you met me?"

I watched in astonishment as she
quickly began to undress in front of me. I
swiftly turned around and faced the wall,
not realizing she was so comfortable getting
naked. "Um, I didn't get *that* vibe from you,
no. I think that was something on my end I
couldn't control." I could hear the
amusement in her voice, and I knew I

looked extremely immature staring at the wall while she tried on clothes.

"You can turn around now," she notified me.

"Did, um, did you like any of them?" I asked as she gathered the clothes up. "Yea, I think I'll get these."

I glanced down at my watch. Greg would be getting home soon. Realizing the time as well, Nia looked back at me and said, "Let me pay for these and I'll walk you to your car."

I was relieved when my car came into view. There was an unsettling feeling dwelling within me, and the calmness Nia managed to have around me was becoming unnerving. "Will I see you tomorrow?" she asked, optimistically. I felt reluctant to answer. Sensing my uncertainty, Nia said, "Mara, I don't want you to be uncomfortable around me. If my sexuality is an issue, let me know."

Guilt took over me as she finished her sentence. I had *no* issues with gay people. *Plenty* of my college friends were gay. Hell, even Porsha had gone through her freshmen bi-curious phase. And the last thing I wanted was for Nia to feel I was uncomfortable around her because of *that*.

I couldn't help but feel the irony at the idea of making sure *Greg's* side chick wasn't uncomfortable thinking *I* had an issue with *her* sexuality.

"It's not that," I said, reassuringly. I watched as Nia stepped closer to me. "What is it?"

Her hazel eyes locked into mine and I felt like my heart was going to explode. My eyes glanced down at her lips, and I felt myself biting mine as I flashed back to our first kiss. "I should go," I breathed out.

But I never moved. Nia's hands were reaching out for my face, but I didn't bother to fight her. I didn't bother to resist. I finally accepted that I wanted her to kiss me. And when our lips finally touched, an adrenaline rush raced through my body, and I found myself pulling her in closer.

Greg

There was a knock at my door, and I was stunned to see my dad in my office doorway. After talking to Ashley a few weeks ago, I began to get nervous when I hadn't been able to get in touch with him. Arthur tried to assure me that he was fine and that he was more than sure it was some kind of mix up on my dad's end. But this was a man who made no mistakes. So it was almost impossible to fight off the thought that there wasn't something going on.

I quickly stood up as my father walked into my office. "Late night for you?"

Everyone else had left for the day, but I decided to stay behind and catch up on one of the contracts he had given me. "Yea, but I'll be wrapping up soon. How was your trip?" He sat down carelessly like he wasn't about to get caught in a lie. "It was something I needed," he responded nonchalantly. Not waiting for me to interrogate him, he stated, "I'm aware I got my dates mixed up with your sister. I decided to head down to our old beach house in Florida since I was in that area."

It was impossible to tell if he was lying or not, and I knew better than to pursue the issue. "Well, I'm glad you were able to take some time off. Was there anything you needed, sir?"

He walked in and sat down at the chair in front of my desk, then motioned for me to sit as well. "I wanted to applaud you on the Dober contract you worked on. The family has decided to use us for all their legal needs."

I calmly nodded my head, though on the inside I was shaking. My father *never* praised me for my work, and I had no idea what was so different now. "Thank you, sir. I'm glad I was able to bring that business to the firm."

I watched as my father eyed my office up and down. I impatiently waited for him to criticize *something* that wasn't to his satisfaction, but his eyes fell back on me. There was a look in them I had *never* seen in my life, and I felt extremely troubled. "Dad, is everything ok?"

I was well aware he wouldn't give me a truthful response. My father was never expressive about his feelings or emotions. Even when my mom died, he kept his composer. He held my sister the entire time she cried but made sure to remind me that *real* men don't shed tears. His silence was beginning to scare me, and the distant look in his eyes didn't make it any better. "Dad?"

"Do you know *why* I'm so hard on you, son?" he finally spoke.

"You want what's best for me," I repeated to him the line I heard from everyone my *entire* life. "You know your grandfather died when I was very young. I had no one around to *teach* me how to be a man. Your grandmother did the best she could, of course, raising five boys by herself. But showing us how to be *men* was the one thing she *couldn't* do."

My eyes never left my father's face as he continued to speak. "I often wonder how many of my brothers would still be alive today if we would've *just* had our father around."

I could feel the emotions within me rising, and I resisted the urge to cry. The majority of my uncles had passed away before I even had a chance to make real memories with them. The only one I could recall was my father's youngest brother who had died right before I started college. He was the victim of a random shooting, although the bullet wasn't meant for him.

And even though I remembered him, the memories were still very few. My dad stayed away from him since every time he was around he asked for money.

"I wasn't the best dad," my father continued, "but I was a father that was there for my family and my son. It's all I knew how to be."

"Dad, where's this coming from?"

I ignored the tears I could see developing within his eyes because I knew my eyes were playing tricks on me. I had been working too hard, staring at my computer screen all day, and now I was seeing things. Because *my* dad *doesn't* cry.

Robinson men *never* cry.

My father cleared his throat and quickly stood up. I watched as he headed towards my office door. I resisted the urge to call out to him, still unsure by everything he had just said to me. He stopped in the doorway and turned back, "When you have a child, Greg, be a *dad* to him, do you hear me? No matter what, be a good dad for your child!"

I nodded as he smirked at me and headed down the hall. It wasn't until I was positive he was gone, did I allow the tears to roll down my face. I wasn't sure what had just happened, and part of me wanted to believe I had made the entire scenario up in my mind.

I picked up the phone to call Mara. I wasn't sure what I was going to say, or if I could even get myself together quickly enough to stop crying. I knew I just *needed* to hear her voice.

"Hi, you've reached Mara Robinson. I am unable to come to my phone right now. Please leave a message and I'll give you a call back at my earliest convenience."

I hung the phone up and shot Keith a text.

"Drinks tonight?"

My phone vibrated back quickly.

"Plans with Kiara. Raincheck?"

I sent him the thumbs up emoji and leaned back in my chair. There was no use trying to work. My head was all fucked up from what took place. It was late where Ashley was, so I wasn't going to call her and bother her with this. Especially since I wasn't even sure what "*this*" was myself. Ashley had always seen a different side of our dad, but even she had *never* seen our dad cry before.

I began to gather my things in hopes that Mara would just be home when I got there. I didn't care if she was already sleeping, I just needed her. I yanked the building door open and saw Nia standing on the other side of the door, smiling.

"Took you long enough!" she said, pleased by the surprised look on my face.

"*What are you doing here?*" I asked, looking around to make sure everyone was gone for the day. "Don't worry, I parked across the street until I saw all the cars leave. No one saw me!" Not waiting for an invite, she walked into the empty office building and sat on the receptionist's desk.

I reluctantly closed the door behind me and turned to face her. "Nia, I was just on my way out. I need to get home!"

She eyed me up and down seductively, and I realized she was wearing a trench coat and heels. She sashayed towards me and wrapped her arms around my neck. "You're free to leave, Mr. Robinson. As soon as you help me with *my* little problem!"

She began to place kisses on my neck and face. I could feel her hands fiddling with the zipper on my pants. "Nia, wait," I said, grabbing her hands. She looked up at me confused. "What's wrong?" I knew I wasn't hiding my emotions very well, but I had no intention of letting her see me break down. She placed her hands on my face and forced me to look at her. "Greg, *what's wrong?*" she asked again.

I could hear the alarm in her voice as I replayed my father's words over and over again in my head. *Men don't cry. Robinson men don't cry!*

Nia continued to stare at me, so worried about what was going on within me. She pulled me in for a hug and whispered, "Its ok, Greg. Whatever it is, it's going to be ok." I could feel the masculinity I had been holding on to for so long begin to dissolve, and the tears without my consent began to fall.

I felt weak.

Pathetic even.

And I could only imagine how disappointed everyone would be if they could see me crying right now. My dad. Ashley. *Mara*.

All of those people who *needed* me to be strong, and here I was, crying into Nia's shoulder. I let my briefcase fall out of my hands, and I drew her in closer to me. She started wiping the tears off of my face and replaced them with kisses. "It's going to be ok, baby. I promise!" Her hazel eyes were now staring into mine. I saw no sense of judgment there, no amount of disgust at this grown-ass black man crying.

There was only sympathy as she looked back at me and I couldn't help but feel aroused by it. I brought her lips to mine and kissed her eagerly. Sensing my readiness, she untied the trench coat she had been wearing, and let it fall to the floor. She was naked. I watched as she walked over to the receptionist's desk, and sat down with her legs wide open. "Come here," she said seductively. "Let me make everything all better!"

Mara

I banged impatiently on Porsha's door, knowing she was awake watching the news. I had zoomed out of the house as soon as Greg left for work and raced over to her house. She opened her door startled by my random pop up, but the look on my face let her know it was serious.

"*You confronted him?*" she asked, as I walked passed her. I began pacing back and forth, not knowing what to say. Or better yet, not knowing *how* to say what I *needed* to say. The words were fumbling around in my head, but I couldn't find the strength to say them out loud. Porsha finally stood in front of me and grabbed both my arms.

"Mara, what's going on?"

I could feel the nauseating feeling creeping within me, and I knew I was going to be sick. But this time, it was word vomit that came out. "*I kissed her!*"

I knew my confession meant nothing to Porsha without the backstory, but she still couldn't help but be shocked. "*Who is her?*"

I made my way to her sofa and sat down. An adrenaline rush was taking over me. "*Her! Nia! I kissed her!*"

I waited for my best friend to yell at me, to question to me, to give me the third degree like she had given people she interrogated for her articles. Instead, she sat down across from me, unsure of what to say. "It was an accident, well, I mean, I *think* it was. I don't think she recognizes me. I don't think she knows who I am."

Porsha's eyes moved back and forth as she struggled to find something to say. She finally looked at me and spoke, "*You kissed your husband's side chick?*"

"*She kissed me!*" I corrected, but we both knew none of that mattered. "Mara, do you realize how *twisted* that sounds?"

"I know! *I know*! I wasn't going to say anything at first, but we've been texting, and we've had lunch a few times, and I don't know. Porsha, I don't know!"

"*You've had lunch with this bitch?* Mara, is Greg cheating making you delusional? *What are you doing?*" And it was a question I had been asking myself since the night Nia first kissed me. And now that we kissed again, I had no idea *what* I was doing anymore.

I could tell Porsha was still looking for some kind of explanation, but I had nothing to give her. I could feel the tears sliding down my face as I wondered how I had ended up here. Sneaking around with Nia, while she was sneaking around with *my* husband.

Porsha was soon at my side, holding me as I cried helplessly into her arms. "*I don't know what I'm doing anymore,*" I admitted. "*When I'm around her, it's like I completely forget about Greg and what they have going on. I feel like as long as she's with me, she's not with him!*"

"But Mara, you *have* to understand how insane that is! And she kissed you? What is she, bi?" I nodded, wiping the tears away. "Although she doesn't prefer labels," I stated. Porsha let out a long sigh and I could tell she was struggling with this information just as much as I was. I had intentionally waited to tell her, hoping something would begin to make sense to me. But in truth, things were getting worse. I was starting to look forward to Greg going to work so I could go see her.

I began to care less about him coming home drunk because I was talking to her while he was out. I had this crazy notion that maybe meeting me made her not want to deal with him anymore. Maybe she was ok with just me. With our friendship.

I was silent too long, and Porsha was now studying me. "There's more to this story, isn't there?"

There was the guilt I had locked away on purpose. But I knew she always saw right through me. "Just a little," I whispered out. Without needing anytime, Porsha jumped up and stared at me. "Mara! You *like* her, don't you?" she accused.

But there was no need for me to answer. She knew the truth. She began pacing back and forth, now laughing. "This is some crazy *shit*, Mara! Like what do you expect me to do with this information?"

"Help me! Tell me something! *Anything*!" I pleaded with her. Though I knew there wasn't much to be said in this scenario. Porsha made her way back by me and sat down. "I can't believe I'm saying this, but Mara, you're going to have to *end* things with *Greg's mistress*, ok?"

There was no need to argue. Porsha was right. I don't know what I was thinking or what my expectations were. But Nia had to go. I would end my friendship, or whatever it was, with her. Then confront Greg. Maybe if he came clean we could get counseling and get through this. I wanted to believe that. To *convince* myself that once Nia was out of the picture we could go back to being how it used to be.

I could feel Porsha's eyes still on me and I closed my eyes and nodded. "You're right. I'll end things with her tonight."

―――――――――――――

Nia opened the door, and the excitement on her face let me know this was going to be harder than I expected. "Mara, come in," she said. I made my way inside her house towards her sofa to sit down.

"What's wrong," she asked me with a sincere look of worry on her face. The tears stung at my eyes, and my heart was all confused. I looked up to see Nia kneeling, her face inches away from mine. "Mara, *please*, whatever it is, just tell me!"

I took in a huge breath, and whispered, "Nia, I can't see you anymore. I don't know *what this is*, but I can't do it!"

I watched as my words impacted her and she began to appear upset as well. Nia stood up and took a few steps back, and I prayed she would say something. *Anything*.

"You feel guilty for being around me?" she asked. The answer was stuck somewhere inside my head, and I had no idea how to respond. On one hand, I *did* feel guilty. I felt guilty about allowing the two of them to continue with this lie. I felt guilty for not calling them out on this sooner. Not confronting them both. I felt guilty for feeling a sense of arrogance every time Nia made time for me because I knew she wasn't spending it with *him*. But there was a new form of guilt I was feeling, and I had no more room for it.

Nia was back in my face, and I turned away from her eyes. I didn't want to change my mind. I didn't want to be that weak. I felt her hand on my face. I could see the same look in her eyes, the same look she had in the bar the first night we met. The same look she had on Magazine Street when she kissed me. I watched as she leaned in, and waited for the familiar touch of her lips against mine.

As the tears slid down my face, I pulled her in closer to me as we kissed. Somehow she had managed to get me on my feet, and I was following her to her bedroom.

As she closed her bedroom door and turned to face me, the realization of what was happening kicked in. She walked towards her bed and I watched as she slowly undressed.

I stood before her, trembling. My legs threatening to betray me at any given moment. *How could she be calm? So relaxed?* I thought, watching this woman standing before me naked. This beautiful, sexy woman who could have *anyone* she wanted, yet her eyes were on me. "Come here," she whispered, and those words sent a jolt of bravery through my body. I felt my hand reaching out for hers. She brought my fingertips to her lips, tracing them slowly, then carefully sucking on each one.

My eyes never once left her face, even as she slid my fingers down in between her breast, past her belly button, and down in between in her legs. "I…I don't know what to do!" I stuttered embarrassingly. But she grinned, so seductively, and said, "Follow my lead!" I could feel every muscle in my body relax as my finger slid inside of her. She was so warm and inviting, I wanted to be deeper and explore more of her. She stared back at me, biting her lip with pleasure as my fingers moved curiously inside of her, basking in the wetness I was currently creating.

She finally grabbed my face, pulling me close to hers, "I want to taste you!"

Shivers ran through me as she unbuckled my jeans. Though I was anxious to feel her tongue on my body, I was disappointed to be removed from inside of her. She spun me around, placing small, aggressive kisses on the back of my neck as she pulled my shirt off. Knowing this might have taken place, I purposely didn't wear a bra, but immediately felt ashamed of my body and covered myself. She whirled me back around to face her and knelt down as she slid my jeans off. She placed kisses on my inner thighs, dragging her nails up and down my legs.

I bit my lip trying to force back the moans that wanted to escape. I could feel every inch of my body begging for her attention, craving for her touch. I couldn't understand how she had gotten me here. How had she seduced me into this erotic state of mind? My head was screaming at me while my heart anticipated this moment. My body completely swept up in lust said, *"Just let go, Mara, just let go!"*

I reached for her hands, stopping her as she made her way in between my legs. She looked up at me with her penetrating hazel eyes and smirked. A cocky smirk and I knew she knew, the battle going on within me. She knew this was wrong and that I couldn't do it. But she knew I would give into her. She was good, *damn* good!

She laid my body down on the bed and as I watched her slide my panty's off, I knew that was it. She had won. And as she made her way inside of me, I let go of all my logical thoughts and gave into my lust. There was no turning back now. I was cheating on my husband . . . *with his own mistress.*

Greg

"What's wrong with dad?"

Ashley didn't even bother to conceal the fear in her voice, and I wondered if he had talked to her. Had he cried to her like he almost did in front of me the other night?

He had went on another trip not too long after our talk but didn't bother telling me. He just sent out a companywide email letting everyone know Arthur was temporarily in charge while he was gone. I, of course, confronted Arthur about my father's whereabouts, but as a loyal friend would, he kept the secret to himself.

"Hello?" Ashley screeched on the other side of the phone. "Yea, I'm here. I, uh, I have no idea what's wrong with dad.

You know that man is as secretive as they come. I'm sure it's just old age. He's feeling bad about retiring or something," I said, trying to convince myself more than her.

Truth was, I felt like *something* was wrong. I had been feeling like that since Ashley called me the first time about my father. And not knowing was becoming scarier than nerve-wracking as the days passed.

"I have to tell you something, Greg. But you can't get mad!"

The cautiousness in her voice instantly made me feel uneasy, and a part of me wanted to tell her to keep it to herself. I didn't want to know. I didn't want to carry that burden with her. But I knew that wasn't fair. I was her big brother. It *was* my burden to carry. "I could never be mad at you, Ash," I responded, hoping to make light of the situation. I knew it was something severe when she didn't acknowledge the nickname she hated.

"A couple of weeks ago, when I went by dad to check on him, and he wasn't home, I went through his mail."

"*Ashley*! Are you serious?!"

I swiftly took a deep breath in, knowing I had already broken my promise. "What did it say," I said, focusing on the root of the issue more than her actions. "Dad's been spending a lot of time at Tulane Hospital. I don't know for what, but he has *a lot* of medical bills. Did you know about this?"

Lie! I thought to myself. *Tell her a lie so she doesn't have to stress about it! She's too far away to be stressed about this!*

I wanted to protect her. Tell her everything was going to be ok. But the reality was, he was her father too. And whatever was going on, she had the right to now.

"Listen, give me a few days to get down to the bottom of this, and I'll call you and let you know what's up, ok?"

"Are you sure?" she asked, and I could tell she wanted to trust me. "I am positive!"

"Hi, you have reached Mara Robinson. I am unable to come to my phone right now. Please leave a message and I'll give you a call at my earliest convenience."

I hung the phone up and turned back to my computer, even though I knew I wasn't going to be working today. I needed to talk to Mara about this. I needed my wife! I held on to this too long and I needed my partner to confide in.

The way you confided in Nia?

I had beat myself up about that for weeks, feeling beyond mortified that I had let her see me like that. That wasn't a moment to share with her! It was a moment I should've shared with my wife! But it was done, and I had to fix everything falling apart in my life. Starting with my marriage. The past few days had been so weird between us. There was a weird vibe she was giving off, and I couldn't figure out the cause of it. I had originally thought it was the whole baby thing, but she indicated that wasn't it.

The constant fear of her finding out about the affair lingered over me, but Mara wasn't the type to stay silent about it. I was *sure* of it.

There was a buzz on my phone from the front desk. "Mr. Robinson, you have a call on line one."

I cleared my throat as I answered the phone, hoping it was my wife. "Gregory Robinson speaking."

"So is this what I'm reduced to? Calling you on your work phone?" A chill shot through me as I recognized Nia's voice. I had been avoiding her since that night, and I was hoping she would soon get the hint. I sincerely felt bad about it, but there was too much going on in my life I needed to focus on. And I needed Nia out of the picture. Keith had instructed I do this face to face, but Nia didn't appear to be the kind of woman you casually walk away from.

"Nia, I'm *really* busy at work. I can't really talk!"

"*Bullshit!*" she shot back at me. "Stop lying to me, Greg. I know you're not busy at work! And stop feeding me bullshit about something being wrong with your wife, I *know* she's fine!"

I couldn't help but look around as if she were possibly watching me. I leaned closer to the phone and began whispering, "Listen, Nia, I have to go." An unfamiliar laugh escaped her lips, and a jolt of uneasiness swept over me. "Gregory Robinson, you figure out a way to see me, before I figure out a way to *see you!* Do you understand?"

Before I had a chance to say anything else, she hung up. I listened to the dial tone in my ear, unsure if that was a threat or not.

———————————

Arthur's head popped up as I softly knocked on his office door. "Late night?" he called out to me. "Always. Looks like my dad was right when he said I was going to have plenty of late nights."

Arthur nodded as he leaned back in his chair, taking his glasses off as he continued to look at me. "It's only because he *knows* you can handle it, you know that."

He gave me a reassuring smile and gestured for me to sit down in the chair across from him.

"That's what you like to tell me," I said walking in and taking a seat. Arthur stood up to the mini-bar next to his desk and poured us both a shot of whatever was in his glass bottle. I didn't bother to object the drink, he would persist anyway. "I tell you that because it's the truth. Your old man may not come to you with his praise, but anyone in earshot knows how proud he is of you!"

We raised our glasses and swallowed down the well-aged whiskey. Arthur took the glass from my hand and placed it back on his bar. "So, what brings you here? I've been reviewing your work, so I know there's no need for any questions."

I knew there was no point in beating around the bush with Arthur, so I came right out and asked, "Is my father sick?"

I had prayed to get some kind of reaction from him. If he acted shocked or caught off guard, I would know my worst assumptions were wrong. But Arthur's expression never changed, and that intensified my concern. "This is about what Ashley discover, isn't it?"

"*You knew?*"

Arthur grabbed an extra chair from his office and slid it next to mine. "When your father got home and realized his mail had been opened, he checked the cameras in his house and discovered your sister had gone through his things."

I wasn't the least bit surprised about my father having cameras in the house, he was cautious like that. I wasn't even surprised that he didn't fuss at Ashley about snooping, he had always been careful not to fuss at her. I was shocked that he didn't at least confront her about what she had seen and try to clarify things to her. He had to have known how this would look. And how upset she would be.

"If he knew she knew, why didn't he say anything to her? Why didn't he tell her everything was going to be ok?"

"I dearly wish I could answer this for you, Greg. But certain secrets aren't mine to tell. All I can say is this, your father is strong. Always has been, always will be! It'll take a whole hell of a lot to bring that man down!"

Though his words were meant to bring relief, they only caused more dread. There was something my father was battling, something he didn't want to tell us just yet. Maybe it's because it was beatable. He was beating whatever it was and didn't want to alarm us in any way. I couldn't help but think about Ashley, and how this was something she should know.

"So, he's going to be ok?" I asked Arthur, knowing his response already. "Of course, Greg," he said on cue. "Your father is going to be just fine." He patted me on the back as I headed out of his office.

I reached for my cell phone, ready to give Ashley a call and tell her about my conversation with Arthur. I could feel the need to vent rising, and I needed to share my concerns with her. I stared down at the picture of her smiling careful and knew she was probably in Atlanta right now, getting ready for some major event she had going on. I thought about how much this new information would haunt her, as she carried a fake smile for everyone. How she would be on the first flight home, potentially losing out on money to be here with dad.

Pushing my needs aside, I sent her a quick text.

"Talked to Arthur! Dad's doing just fine!"

Mara

"Mara, don't you look stunning," Mr. Robinson complimented. I embraced him and placed a loving kiss on his cheek. "How are you doing?" I asked him. He patted his heart softly. "The old ticker is hanging in there, so I'm doing well! You make sure you enjoy yourself tonight and save me a dance!"

It was my father-in-law's annual company party, and it felt good to be all dressed up and out with Greg. It had been a week since I had slept with Nia. And a week since I had ended things between us. I was shocked that I had taken it as hard as I did. It had taken me longer to get out of the bed in the mornings, and I no longer had the motivation to get through my days since I knew I wasn't going to see her for lunch.

I was ashamed when Greg had noticed it himself. I didn't know if she ended things with him as well, but he started coming home earlier to be with me, and though it felt great having him around, I wondered what Nia was doing.

"There's my beautiful wife." I smiled back at him as he handed me a glass of champagne. He looked amazing tonight, and there was a strong part of me longing to feel him touching me again. It had been so long since we made love, and tonight I desperately needed it. He placed an affectionate kiss on my forehead as we made our way to our table.

Mr. Robinson was already standing in front of our table, chatting with a woman. I could feel Greg's body stiffen as the woman turned around, and my heart dropped.

"And you've already met my son, Miss. Comeaux. This is his beautiful wife, Mara Robinson."

Nia's hazel eyes shifted from my face, then to Greg's. I couldn't bear to look up at my husband out of fear that we would both have the same awkward look on our faces. And yet, Nia remained cool. She reached out and shook Greg's hand casually. "Yes, Greg, it's *so* good to see you again. And Mrs. Robinson, you look *magnificent!*"

I could feel a knot forming and I desperately wanted to excuse myself. But I didn't know what Nia was up to, and I refused to leave my husband's side. "Thank you, Miss Comeaux, you look very beautiful yourself."

There was a look on her face I had never seen before. A look I couldn't read, and it bothered me so much trying to figure out what she was doing here.

There was a different vibe with her tonight, and it was frightening. Had she come here to confront the both of us? Had she come here to call me and Greg out on our infidelity? I could feel my head spinning and I had no choice but to excuse myself and got to the bathroom.

"I'll be right back!"

The wife in me screamed to stand by my husband. But the feelings I had for Nia were overwhelming, and she won.

I shot Porsha a quick text letting her know what was going on and leaned over the toilet as I waited for anything to come up. My phone rang and I quickly answered.

"*Are you kidding me? Is she really fucking there?*" Porsha screeched from the other end. I nodded even though I knew she couldn't see me. "Yes, she introduced herself to me as if it was *nothing*! Like we have *never* met one another!"

The stall around me felt like it was getting smaller and smaller. My dress was clinging to me and I needed to get out of it immediately. "Where are you?" Porsha asked, clearly hearing my mini-panic attack from over the phone. "In the bathroom. I think I'm going to be sick!"

"Mara, I *need* you to pull yourself together and get your ass back by Greg! I don't know what this female is up to, but you *need* to be strong right now!" I allowed Porsha's words to sink in, knowing she was right. This woman had manipulated me *and* my husband enough. I was done.

I headed towards our table, seeing a very angry and uncomfortable look on Greg's face. He and Nia were discussing something, and though he looked upset, she remained calm.

"Everything ok here," I stated, instead of asking Greg jumped at the sound of my voice and quickly wrapped an arm around me. "Everything's great now that you're back," he said, convincingly. I could see a pleased look on Nia's face and knew she was gaining some kind of sick satisfaction seeing me and my husband squirm because of her. I decided to end this right here.

"Miss Comeaux, we would love to stay and *entertain* you this evening, but I *must* get my husband home. I've been dying for some alone time with him. You understand, right?"

Not giving her a chance to respond, I gestured for Greg to follow me.

———————————

The car ride home was long and silent. Though I was proud of how I handled things, the urge to check my phone kept nagging me. *Would she text me and apologize? Would she explain to me why she had been there? Would she finally come clean about it all?*

Greg concentrated firmly on the road, though there was clearly something on his mind. The wife in me wanted to ask, wanted to know why he was so affected by seeing her. But the side of me that had gotten close to Nia understood. And the last thing I needed to hear was his feelings towards a woman I had feelings for too.

I was beyond relieved when our house came into view. But I knew there was nothing that could've been done to salvage this night.

Greg lay in the bed, eyes glued to the ceiling and I had no urge to comfort him. I was busy battling my own emotions. I missed her and seeing Nia tonight made me realize I was dealing with none other than a broken heart. And as I thought these words, I felt even more foolish. I was lying next to a man, who had broken his vows to me, missing his mistress.

Missing her company. Her laugh. Her smile. Her touch. Her kiss.

Missing her voice in my ear telling me how she had wanted to make love to me since she saw me. How attentive she was to my body's responses. I could feel the arousal in me growing, and I couldn't help but arch my back towards Greg, hoping he would respond accordingly.

I could feel his body turn to me, pulling me closer. Our eyes met, and he looked just as lost as I felt. I closed my eyes as he kissed me, trying to imagine Nia's lips instead. I imagined his aggressive, but soft touch was hers. As his body climbed on top of me, I tried to pretend it was Nia. I kept my hands down, knowing if I touched him, the image I had of her curvy body would be ruined.

I could feel his hardness against me, and immediately felt turned off. But I needed this. I needed her. Breaking my concentration, I looked up at my husband and as he tried to remove his pants. "No, just taste me," I whispered, trying to sound seductive. I could care less how it made him feel, I closed my eyes and braced myself as his tongue slid inside of me. The tongue that had made me melt, and cum, so many times before. And as he took his time to please me, I continued to imagine that tongue was Nia's.

Greg

I slammed her front door violently, bounding into her living room. I saw her stunned face as I stood over her. *"What the fuck was that, Nia? Showing up at my job's party like that, knowing my wife would be there!"*

Realizing what I was pissed about, Nia crossed her legs and folded her arms. "I complimented her, *didn't I?"* she said, sarcastically. I could feel my temper getting the best of me and I grabbed the glasses from her coffee table and slammed them to the floor. "You could have ruined *everything*, Nia! Don't you realize that?" I could tell she could careless and I wondered what kind of woman I was truly dealing with.

"I played it cool, Greg, if anyone was suspicious, it was *you*!" A laugh escaped her lips as she looked me up and down, "If your wife didn't know you were having an affair before, she must have *some* kinda clue now!"

"This isn't funny, Nia! This is my *marriage* you're fucking with!" Nia stood up and made her way towards me angrily, "No, Greg! *You're* fucking with *your* marriage! You started fucking with it the day you *fucked* me! *Right here*, on this very sofa! You started *fucking* with it every day after that when you *continued* to *fuck* me!"

Remorse rushed through me as I realized she was absolutely right. This was all on me. Not her, and it was ending. *Now*. She placed her hands around my face trying to calm me down. "Greg, I'm sorry I put you in that situation, ok. It'll never happen again." The confused look on Mara's face replayed in my head and how distant she was when we got home after the party. I made love to her, but it was almost as if neither one of us were into it.

I grabbed Nia's hands and removed them from my face. "You're absolutely right, Nia. This will *never* happen again."

"Why do you sound like that?"

I knew she could read my face clearly, and she knew I was ending this. She shook her head as she stepped back. "*No!* Don't you dare! *Don't you dare tell me it's over between us!*"

I gulped down the knot forming in my throat. I needed to go to Mara. I needed to come clean and pray for forgiveness. I walked away from Nia's hysterical screams and headed to her front door.

"Damnit, Greg, *I'm pregnant!*"

My entire body froze and I prayed I heard her incorrectly. Seeing I wasn't moving, she walked over pulling a pregnancy test out her back pocket. She dropped it in my hands. I stared down at the two pink lines that were slapping me in the face. *Pregnant.*

I handed her the pregnancy test back, not knowing what my next move was supposed to be. What was I supposed to say?

"And *yes*, it's *yours* before you try and go there with me," Nia spat out, clearly hurt by my silence. But what was she expecting? What did she *think* I was going to do in this situation?

"Nia, I...I don't know what you want me to do right now!" I admitted. I could see Mara's face so vividly in my mind. My entire marriage flashed before my eyes and I knew this was going to change everything.

"I want you to man up and help me raise this child!" she demanded. I covered my face as I wondered how I would tell Mara. Did I need to tell her? Maybe I could pay Nia off and sweep this entire situation under the rug. But I knew better. Nia would never let that happen.

"I need to talk to my wife, Nia. I need to explain this situation to her so I can see what our next move needs to be."

"You didn't *need* to consort with her when you were fucking me, Greg! *Why are you talking to her now?*"

"I *need* to explain everything to her to see if my marriage can survive this!"

Nia's eyes began to bulge and I realized I said the wrong thing. I held my arm over my face as she lashed out, punching me anywhere she could. "*Are you fucking kidding me? I'm carrying your child! Not her! Why the fuck would you still want to be with her?*"

I grabbed Nia's arms and pinned them down to her side. "Nia, I *love* my wife! You know I do! *I'm not leaving her!* I'll make sure you and my child are well taken care of! I'll be a part of my child's life! But I am *not* leaving my wife!"

When I was sure she wasn't going to hit me again, I released my grip on her. Tears were streaming down her face and I realized I would break two hearts in one night. I turned to walk to the door, trying to figure out how I was going to tell Mara this. How was I going to fix this?

"Greg," Nia whispered out after me. I stopped at the door and turned to face her. She made her way towards me, wiping the tears away.

"If you don't leave her, Greg. I'm not keeping this baby!"

She was avoiding my eye contact, but the look on her face let me know she wasn't kidding. "If you don't end things with her, and come back to me, *tonight,* I *will* abort this baby!"

———————————

Mara was getting out of the shower when I got home. I watched as she towel-dried her hair, smiling at me from the mirror. "You ok?" she asked. But I couldn't speak. All I could do was stand there, watching her. She walked out of the bathroom looking afraid, and I'm sure I wasn't giving her any indication that everything was ok.

"Greg, talk to me."

I grabbed both her hands and eased her down so she could sit on the bed. I could feel the tears stinging at my eyes, but I had to man up. I had to get through this. "Mara, you know…you know I love you right?"

I could see the fury take over her face, and her eyes began to tear up. "You're cheating on me, aren't you?" she sobbed out. But her tone let me know she already knew the answer to that question. I put my head down and nodded. I couldn't see the look in her eyes when I admitted it. I just couldn't.

I could feel her fists making contact with me as she began fiercely punching me. "You bastard! *You fucking bastard!* I knew it! I fucking *knew* it!" I stood up and she was up next to me, still punching me in my back as I walked away.

"I hate you! *I fucking hate you*! I want you out of my house! *Leave!*"

I grabbed my duffle bag from the top of the closet and began shoving clothes inside of it.

"*Oh you're leaving,*" she continued to scream. "*You're going to her? You're going be with that bitch?*"

"Yes!" I yelled out.

Her punches stopped and I finally turned to face her. Tears covered her entire face, and I watched as the impact from my words caused her to collapse to the floor. She was clutching her chest and I wanted to reach down and hold her. Tell her everything was going to be ok. The tears slid down my face as I zipped my bag up and walked passed her. "Greg," she called after me. I stopped by the bedroom door, refusing to turn around. She didn't deserve this, she didn't deserve *any* of this.

I could feel her eyes on my back and I knew what she wanted. What she needed. She needed me to scoop her off the floor and tell her it was all a lie. That everything was going to be ok. But I couldn't do that. Nia was waiting for me. I had to leave. "Greg, I love you," she sobbed out.

"I love you too, Mara. I always will."

Mara

I was completely overwhelmed with rage and my hands trembled as I banged on her front door. The tears stung at my eyes and I felt like this lie had gone on long enough. It had been an interesting and erotic experience in the beginning but it was over now and I was done playing her game.

"Mara, what's wrong?" Nia asked, a convincing look of sincerity taking over her face. Her stupid face that I had fallen for! I wanted to reach out and choke her. Choke her till she was no longer breathing. Choke her so I wouldn't have to hear the lies she was about to tell.

Or maybe for once, the truth! God, how I didn't want to hear the truth either!

I rushed inside her home, expecting to see Greg casually sitting on her sofa.

Expecting to see the shocked look on his face when he realized I too was fucking his side chick! He was nowhere in sight.

Had I beaten him here? Was he hiding somewhere?

I ran my fingers through my hair, pulling at it, trying to find sanity in this situation. Nia's eyes never left me. She looked scared and panicked.

Had they not talked? Had Greg not told her he told me everything?

"You're starting to scare me, Mara, talk to me! What's wrong?"

She reached out for me, but I backed away quickly. "Don't touch me, don't you ever *fucking* touch me!" Nia looked at me with discomfort in her eyes and folded her arms. She put her head down no longer wanting to look at me and for some twisted reason *I* felt guilty for talking to her that way. I was feeling guilty for hurting *her.*

The urge to laugh at the irony of that crossed my mind. But it hurt too much right now to laugh. Plus I wouldn't let her get to me like that! I wouldn't let her manipulate me any longer. "*Fuck you!*" I screamed. "**Fuck you for doing this to me! For making me feel this way, knowing all along who I was, and what you were doing!**"

She looked back up at me as if making sure it was ok to speak, "Mara, I'm sorry you feel guilty about what's happened between us, but I'm not going to apologize for my feelings for you. I genuinely care about you and your happiness!"

Though her words meant *everything* to me, I knew they were lies.

"You're a liar! You wanted to fuck me for your own gain! You are a sick and twisted individual, and I don't know what kind of sick games you and Greg are playing but I wish the best to you both!"

I was rushing to the door when she grabbed me, "Mara, I don't know *what the hell* is going on but I've done everything in my power to show you how I feel about you! I care about you, and I'm nothing like your husband, you know that!" I shoved her arms off me and screamed, *"YA'LL ARE JUST ALIKE! BOTH FUCKING WITH MY EMOTIONS, DRAINING ME! WELL, I'M DONE! YA'LL CAN HAVE EACH OTHER, YA'LL DESERVE EACH OTHER!"*

I tried rushing passed her again, but she continued to block the door. "Mara, what the *fuck* are you talking about? *Have each other? What?*"

She was *too* good at this, and it was driving me nuts. I wiped the tears from my eyes and forced myself to calm down. "I know about you and Greg, *Shania*! You've been *sleeping* with my husband for *months* now! I've *seen* the two of you together! Don't lie to me anymore!" Her eyes widened and she finally knew, I knew the truth. I watched as she walked slowly towards her sofa and sat down.

My body urged for me to leave, but my anger glued me to the floor. I was waiting for her to laugh, to say, "You caught me!" but she looked just as jumbled as I felt.

"Why...why would you be around me, if you knew I was sleeping with your husband?" she asked. And just like that, the guilt was back on me. She turned and faced me, my silence concerning her. "Why would you befriend me? Care about me, if you knew I was sleeping with your husband? Were you playing with my feelings?"

"NO," I yelled out quickly.

"When I found out about you, I *needed* to know what it was about *you* that made him want to cheat! Why had he chosen *you* over *me*! You seemed so genuine and so sweet. And when you kissed me I wanted to forget that you were this horrible person, destroying my marriage! I wanted to *believe* you were here for me!"

I couldn't help but laugh at my own words. Here I was with the woman my husband was leaving *me* for, practically begging her to love me and not him. But I already knew the outcome of this. Greg made it clear our marriage was over and he wanted to be with her. I just didn't know what hurt worse. Losing her to him, or him to her.

I watched her reach for her phone and walk towards me. "Do you care about me, Mara?" she asked and I could feel my heart stop.

Was this some kind of trick? Was she setting me up just to laugh at how she was able to manipulate me all this time?

Her question stabbed like a knife in my heart, but I heard myself say, "Yes, Shania, I care about you!" And the tears began to drop.

I didn't fight her this time as she embraced me. I allowed myself to break down and cry, to be weak with her while she kept herself together. I allowed us to have this moment because I knew it would be our last. She pulled away from me with a sly grin on her face as she went through her phone. I rolled my eyes wondering if she was calling him, or if she had been recording the conversation the entire time. I kicked myself at the image of them sitting together, laughing at how they had both managed to destroy me. *Again*!

Finally, she turned her phone towards me and said, "My name's *Ania*, my *sister's* name is *Shania*!"

I immediately felt dizzy as I grasped Nia's phone.

There were *two* of them!

Twins!

Identical twins!

Nia was a twin.

I looked back and forth as if it were an illusion! Another evil trick being played upon me, but I continued scrolling through pictures and there were more and more of them, going back to them as kids. I looked back up at her as she wiped my tears away.

"I'm *not* the one having an affair with *your* husband, Mara. My *twin sister is!*"

Shania

I rolled my eyes as I sent Kissy to voicemail for the fifth time. I don't know *what* she wanted, but I didn't care. Greg was at my house, *finally*, in the shower. I had decided to go and pick us up something to eat and grab a bottle of wine. Though I wouldn't be drinking. I could tell the conversation with his wife didn't go well, so I intended to show him how appreciative I really was that he was *finally* mine!

An annoyed grunt escaped my lips as I finally answered the phone, "For Christ's sake, *what*, Kissy? *Are you dying? Is Nana dead?* Cause something serious better be going on for you to be blowing up my phone!"

"You're sleeping with a married man?" she attempted to ask, but from the tone of her voice, I could hear the accusation.

How in the fuck?

"Kissy what are you talking about?"

"Don't *bullshit* me, Nia. You know, I know you too well for that."

Damn twin connection.

I don't know how she figured it out, but I had no intention of dealing with her judgments right now. That's why I had kept Greg away from her! Once she spotted us together, she would've *immediately* known we were sleeping together.

The one thing about being twins I *always* hated. I wondered how long it would take for her to figure out I was pregnant, especially since she had started feeling sick lately. I thought she would've realized it not too long after almost puking at my house the other day. But hell, I didn't even realize I was pregnant then!

"Kissy, what *I* do has *nothing* to do you with you! You'll be back in Florida soon, where you *want* to be! And I'll be here, continuing with *my life* as I always do. So, if this is a call to make me feel guilty, don't waste your time. I'm in love and I *will be* happy!"

"And while you're happy, another woman's heart is breaking!" Kissy lectured. I could feel the anger in me rising.

"*Seriously*, Kissy? For *once* can you put your sister *first*? What about *me* and my *happiness*? Can you for *once* think about me before worrying about some random woman you don't even know?"

"Nia I have *always* cared about your happiness! But for whatever reason, you think I'm out to get you!"

I gripped the steering wheel wishing it was Kissy's neck. "You've *never* cared about me, Kissy! Ever since we were little, you've done *everything* in your power to make sure I was unhappy!"

"*HOW, Nia*? What did I do that was *so* horrible to you as a child that makes you feel that way?"

I had finally had enough of this!

"*You took mama and daddy away from us, Kissy! Because of YOU, mama and daddy are dead, and Nana had to raise us!*"

There was complete silence on the other end, and I knew there was no way she could apologize out of this one. "Is *that* why you hate me, Nia? Because of mama and daddy?" I could hear the hurt in her voice and it made me want to laugh. How *dare* she be hurt behind something *she* caused!

"Yes, Kissy! Because you just couldn't keep your *damn* mouth shut, we lost everything! Daddy, Mama, our home. Everything I knew and loved was taken away from ME *because of you!*"

"*Nia*...daddy was *molesting* us! What did you *want* me to do?"

I forced the flashbacks of my father sneaking into our room out of my mind. I wouldn't allow Kissy to flip this scenario around. Yes, what he did was wrong. But I *knew* he'd eventually stop. And it wasn't relevant what he did in the dark, during the daytime we were a family! We were happy!

Till Kissy felt the need to tell a teacher at school what was going on.

Daddy got arrested and sent to jail. He didn't last a full month in prison before they found him hanging from his neck in his cell. Mama couldn't handle the guilt of not knowing and soon overdosed on something not too long after he died.

And then Nana stepped up and took us in. I *loved* Nana has a child. Always loved going over there, but when I saw how she treated Kissy, knowing it was *her* fault Nana's only child was dead, I was furious! How could Nana love her, when she was the reason daddy was gone? How could she forgive her?

How could I forgive her?

"Nia, *I'm sorry* that after all these years you blame me for what happened to our parents. I'm sorry. But I wanted it to stop. I wanted the pain he caused us to just *stop*!"

Kissy was crying uncontrollably into the phone and I could feel the tears stinging in my eyes. But I wouldn't cry, not for her. I'd *never* cry for her. I'd cry for the childhood I missed out on, because of her. The parents that would never see the child I was carrying, *because of her*!

I could feel the fury inside of me consuming every ounce of my being, and before she had the chance to say anything else, I hung up. Sister or *not*, I *hated* her. She always had a way of ruining my moment. She was still blowing my phone up, clearly wanting to get off her chest *whatever* she wanted to say. But I didn't want to hear. Hear, read, or even allow her to leave it on a voicemail. I knew she'd probably tell Nana, but I didn't care what her opinion was either. I wasn't going to let them destroy this for me.

Yea, I was quite aware Greg's precious wife would be heartbroken by him leaving her. But she'd get over it! And so would Greg after our baby was born. I was never much of a baby person, I personally never liked kids. But seeing the look in Greg's eyes when I told him he was going to be a daddy, made this all worth it. If I was lucky, we'd be able to hire a nanny so I wouldn't have to deal with the child as much.

Kissy's name was still popping up on my phone and I knew the only way I'd get some peace is to cut her out of my life *completely*! I quickly grabbed my phone and went to my call log to block her. Maybe I would deal with her tomorrow, but tonight was my night, and nothing was going to ruin that!

I was so distracted, fooling around with my phone, I didn't notice my car swerve into another lane. I *never* saw the car driving towards me. Only heard the blaring of its horn, and then finally felt the impact as the car smashed into mine.

One Year Later

Mara

Kissy held my hand tightly as we walked into the attorney's office. I never in my life thought I would step back into this building again. But when Arthur called me, I knew it was a legal matter I couldn't ignore. Ashley had called me two weeks ago, letting me know her father had died. A courtesy I was grateful for. Apparently, Mr. Robinson had silently been fighting lung cancer, but he soon lost the battle.

And though she *begged* me to come to the funeral, the idea of running into Greg was something I wasn't ready for. But clearly, the universe felt differently, because here we were, the day after his father's funeral, about to be sitting across from one another.

"Would you like me to take him?" Kissy asked, reaching for my son, Brandon.

After everything had come out, Nia and Kissy being twins, and Greg's affair, I shockingly found out *I was pregnant.* A blessing from the universe for everything that I had been through, I assumed. I didn't know I was going to have the strength to get through Greg leaving me. But once I saw Brandon's face on the ultrasound for the first time, I knew nothing else mattered besides him.

I thankfully handed Brandon to Kissy just as Greg and Nia entered the room. I wasn't the least bit surprised to see her smiling at me smugly as she held Greg's hand. Kissy had told me about her miscarriage after the car accident she had gotten into, and how she'd never be able to carry a child of her own. I felt sorry for her loss, though I never sent my condolences.

"*Sister*," Nia said sarcastically towards Kissy. I felt terrible that their relationship had only gotten worse since everything happened. Nana ended up selling her house and moving to Florida with us, causing an even bigger rift between them. But Kissy made it clear that though they were twins, they never *really* had a sisterly bond.

"Hello, Nia," Kissy said back politely. I placed a soothing hand on her leg.

Greg was sitting across from me, and though I was still disappointed in how our marriage ended, my heart ached for him. I ignored the decision to remain silent and spoke to him, "I'm *truly* sorry for your loss, Greg. Your father was a *great* man, and very well-loved!"

I could see the stunned look in his eyes as he finally looked up at me. "Thank...thank you. How's Brandon?"

His eyes fell helplessly on our son. The son *he* decided not to be there for since Nia had him completely locked down. I had tried to do the right thing and notify him about the doctor's appointments, the baby shower, even when I went into labor. And though everyone told me how crazy I was, I felt he still deserved to know. There were moments, when I looked at the magnificent life *we* created and wondered how Greg could stay away from him. But in the end, it was a burden he would have to carry on his own.

Arthur finally walked in and the tension in the room lightened up a bit. "Hello, Arthur," Nia said, standing up to embrace him. "It's so good to see you again? How's Samantha and the grandkids?" Arthur looked from me to Nia, slightly uncomfortable. "They're all doing fine," he answered unsurely. Nia continued to smile, "That's wonderful. We'll all have to grab lunch after this!"

Arthur nodded and gestured for her to sit down. He took his seat at the head of the table and turned to me. "Hello, Mara, it's been so long!" I gave him a polite smile, understanding the difficulty of the situation he found himself in.

"It has been, but I am glad you were able to make it to the shower. Brandon adores the car seat you bought him!" I tried not to feel too satisfied with the look of betrayal on Nia's face, but after *everything* she had put me through, I felt I deserved to gloat just a little at her dissatisfaction with knowing some of Greg's friends still kept in touch with me.

"Shall we begin?" Arthur asked pulling paperwork out of his briefcase. Nia cleared her throat demanding everyone's attention. "With all due *respect*, Arthur, this is the reading of Greg's *father's* will. I'm not too sure why his *ex-wife* needs to be here."

Arthur separated the documents before responding. "With all due respect, *Shania*, Greg, and Mara were still legally married when Mr. Robinson drafted the last version of his will, and it just so happens Miss Mara is in it." I could see the surprised looks on Greg and Nia's faces, and could barely hide the astounded one on mine. Though I had kept in touch with Mr. Robinson over the months, I *never* expected he'd leave me *anything*.

"Should we wait for Ashley?" Nia asked. "Miss Ashley and I spoke on yesterday since she had to fly back out after the funeral. She'll be back later on in the week to finalize all matters. Now, I won't make this a drawn-out matter, so we'll start with you, Greg. Your father is leaving his estate for you and your sister to divide evenly unless one of you intends to keep the home. Ms. Ashley has no intention of moving back, as she made clear to me, so she's all for the house being sold."

"Your father also left you a portion of his percentage of the company, raising your percentage from twenty-five to forty-one percent." Greg's head snapped up as he looked at Arthur as if there was some mistake.

"*Forty-one*? That's not even half, Arthur!!" Arthur just reread the documents as if the wording would change. He finally slid the paper over to Greg to read himself.

"Your father's words, not mine. As for Miss Mara," Arthur said turning to me, "Mr. Robinson said he knew how much you admired his beach house in Florida and he's leaving it to you!" I could feel myself tearing up. It would be hard going to that house knowing there were so many memories there with Greg. But I looked forward to the new ones I could create with Kissy and Brandon. Kissy squeezed my shoulder, giving me a cheering smile.

"He also left behind a few of Mrs. Robinson's jewelry in a safety deposit box located at Chase Bank, for you to do as you please with. As for his *one* and *only* grandchild, Brandon Robinson, he leaves behind the rest of his percentage of the business. Including the partial businesses he owns in Baton Rouge, Lafayette, and Beaumont."

We all jumped as Nia slammed her hand down. "*That's bullshit.* He's a *baby* and *can't* do anything with that!"

Arthur held his finger up, "Mr. Robinson was aware of that. It states here until Mr. Brandon becomes of age, all business matters are to be held by his legal guardian, Mara Robinson."

I felt my heart stop as Arthur said my name. Hearing Kissy squeal confirmed what he had said was factual, and that I wasn't losing my mind. I stared at Arthur blankly as he looked back at me smiling. "Are, are you *serious?*" I stuttered out. I looked down at Brandon coo'ing affectionately in Kissy's arms. He was a *business owner.*

My little boy is a business owner!

I could feel the hot tears slide down my face and I wasn't the least bit embarrassed. I stood up and placed kisses all over Kissy and Brandon's faces. Arthur stood up and reached for my hand proudly. "I look forward to working for you, Miss Mara." Wiping my tears away I shook his hand and laughed.

Nia slammed her hands against the table as she stood up. "This is *bullshit,* Arthur! Greg deserves that percentage and you know it!"

Arthur had placed the paperwork back into his briefcase. "It matters not what I *think*, but what Mr. Robinson *wanted*." I watched as she walked around the table to put her face near mines. It amazed me how she and Kissy were identical, yet she was *so* ugly to me.

"*Please* believe Greg and I will take you to court! If Brandon is a partial owner of the firm, he belongs with his *father*! I swear we'll get full custody, and leave you and my sister with *nothing*!"

Before I could speak, Arthur was at my side. "*Please do*, Miss Comeaux. *Please* take her to court, so I can represent her, and make sure her son *owns* the *entire* company by the time I'm done!"

Nia's eyes glared at the both of us. Realizing she had *at last* been defeated, she whirled around and barked at Greg that she was ready to go.

I watched as the man I was once so proud to call my husband, stood up with his head down, also looking defeated. As he reached for the doorknob he turned back to look at his son. "I'd *really* like to spend time with him if that's possible."

As badly as I wanted to hurt him, I knew I couldn't, and there was no point trying. He had given me my son, and everything he had ever wanted, I now had. I smiled sincerely at him, "I'm sure we can arrange something." He gave me a thankful smile and headed out the door.

I turned back and saw Kissy looking at me astonished. "You're a *way* better woman than me, Mara. I would have given his ass the blues!"

I smiled as I scooped Brandon into my arms. "There was no need to bruise his ego anymore. I think he learned a very valuable lesson today. Cheater's *never* prosper."

———————————————

HA!

Guys, we did it! Book TWO! Can you believe it? I know I am still in shock, but extremely grateful!

I *have* to continue to thank you guys for your support, your feedback, and your love!

I simply write these stories, you guys make it all worth it!

So, of course, I have to give you guys a little sample of book three (YES THERE'S A THREE)!

It's the least I can do for your support! Please keep the feedback coming and let me know what you think! Your opinions are very valuable to me!

I hope you enjoyed Cheater's Never Prosper, and really hope you like the sneak peek of book three:

Confessions of a Side Chick
By: Leina Duncan

Introductions

Porsha

I'm not sure where the term "side chick" came from, but I know I've dealt with my fair share of infidelities to have a personal dislike towards them. I've been called, text, DM'd, even had women bold enough to approach me on the street to let me know the man I *thought* was mine, *wasn't*. I've seen relationships, and marriages, crumble and fall because one person simply couldn't be faithful and allowed another to sabotage what they had spent years building.

I was one of *many* women blasting Monica's "Sideline Ho" when it dropped, dedicating it to all the scandalous women out there who preyed on taken men.

Women who I believed were conniving, vindictive, and had *no* self-worth. Women I wrote off as having no morals, no goals, and no integrity. Sure, some women existed who simply did not know about the wife/girlfriend. Women who genuinely may have been a victim to a man's smooth talk and lies. But then there are the others, who know and see your relationship, and those women just don't care. And though at one point in my life, Monica's song defined everything I needed to know about a side chick, unfortunately now, I have to disagree.

As amazing as that song is, I'm realizing now, it only reflected one side of the story, and though there's no argument that it was the best side, it wasn't the only one that needed to be told.

Yes, as a side chick you are second and you are limited. You spend nights alone, waiting for the moment he's free to call or text you. You lay awake at night wondering if he kisses her like he kisses you; is he touching her like he touches you. It's nerve-racking and honestly downright sad. But one thing that song failed to caption, and the one thing the rest of the world forgets to focus on was the role that *man* plays in this whole set up.

See, women, as smart and as strong as we want to be, are outright stupid when we're in love. Just like you find the strength within you to stay with his cheating ass, side chicks find that weakness to stay with his taken ass.

And as wrong as it feels to be a side chick to a married man, or a man in a relationship when your hearts involved, you'll do a whole lot of wrong to be with that man!

Desiree

I'm the girl you see in the club and automatically pull your man closer to you for security. And though this has always brought me much amusement, if I saw me, I would do the exact same thing. See, I learned at an early age how men think and how they operate! No, this isn't some sob story about me getting my heart broken, cause that for damn sure isn't the case! I've never given the man the satisfaction of having my heart, and I damn sure never will.

See, I'm the woman you want to label with all these negative stereotypes, "She's a hoe cause she's sleeping with a married man!" And that's fine! Think that way, because just like I know men, I know women better! It's so easy for us to pass judgment on the next woman and the moves she makes just to appease our own frame of mind. You want to categorize and belittle me because

I'm making moves you don't have the confidence to make! So, in all actuality, you 'wifeys' should be thanking me!

You see, when a man says he wants "a lady in the streets and a freak in the sheets," you simple-minded women thought he was referring to just one woman!

And I'm sorry, I *have* to laugh at that one*! No ladies*! He wants a trophy wife he can parade around in public, and that freak he can fuck in the bathroom while his trophy is waiting at the bar, clueless. And I am glad to say, *I am that freak*!

I'm the reason your husband or boyfriend comes home to you at night! I'm the reason your man stays although he's not fully satisfied. See, I'm not one of these chicks trying to *take* your man, trust me, honey, I don't want him. I see firsthand what he's putting you through, *why would I want that drama?*

I'm a different breed of a female! I'm the chick he vents to when he's not happy at home! I'm the chick that gives him advice on how to deal with you! I'm the chick picking out your birthday and Christmas gifts because he needs a woman's touch! I'm the chick that doesn't call or text first, because I know he's with you! I'm the chick that can walk straight past him while he's with you, and never bat an eye his way. I'm the chick he'll never get caught up with because I know how to move in silence.

And you can sit here and turn your noses up all you want because your judgments have never bothered me. Nor does it pay my bills! Oh, but did I forget to mention that your man does?

Books by Leina Duncan:

Something Like Cupid

Cheater's Never Prosper

Coming soon:

Confessions of a Side Chick

Printed in Great Britain
by Amazon

21696882R00169